Ernst von Wildenbruch

The Master of Tanagra

an artist's story of Old Hellas

Ernst von Wildenbruch

The Master of Tanagra
an artist's story of Old Hellas

ISBN/EAN: 9783337387969

Printed in Europe, USA, Canada, Australia, Japan

Cover: Foto ©Andreas Hilbeck / pixelio.de

More available books at **www.hansebooks.com**

THE MASTER OF TANAGRA.

An Artist's Story of Old Hellas.

BY

ERNST VON WILDENBRUCH.

TRANSLATED FROM THE SEVENTH GERMAN EDITION BY THE

BARONESS VON LAUER.

New Edition, Illustrated with Twenty-Five Tanagra Figures.

LONDON:

H. GREVEL AND CO., 33, KING STREET, COVENT GARDEN, W.C.

1887.

PREFACE.

AMONGST the most noteworthy of the day must be ranked incontestably the poetic productions of Ernst von Wilden-bruch. Poetic fervour and powerful conception, combined with pure classic style, imparting that grace and beauty of form which touch the heart, and transport far away from every-day life into the ideal world, under the magic sway of the good, the beautiful, and the true — these are the prime characteristics that distinguish him above the foremost. The works of this celebrated German poet should surely become familiar in every cultivated society that takes active interest in the intellectual life of our times.

The present story refers to "The Master of Tanagra," the mythical sculptor of the charming little figures found at Tanagra; and affords a reflex of old Greek life, its ways and

teachings, combines much dramatic incident,
and brings the chief personages—Praxiteles,
Phryne, Myrrholus, and Hellenofila—before
the mind's eye in vivid reality. The scene
alternates from Tanagra to Athens. Art is
the motor which causes Myrrholus to leave
the land of his adoption: but love is the
cause of his return, finding his proper sphere,
and becoming "Master of Tanagra."

The fascination produced by the Tanagra
figures is not caused solely by the real Grecian
grace, with which the most simple situations
and motives gleaned from reality have been
retained and fixed in plastic form, but is
chiefly the consequence of the unspeakably
delicate tones applied, which seem to play
around them like a zephyr. There can be
no doubt that these precious reproductions
will receive unqualified praise at the hands
of all supporters of art.

THE MASTER OF TANAGRA.

"TANAGRA will quickly be reached, and the most beautiful part of our journey lies ahead ! " said a crisp-haired, slenderly-built man, hailing from the northern outlet of Oropos, a townlet on the borders of Attica and Bœotia, as he swung himself into the travelling-car beside his companion.

The goad was dashed against the flanks of the horses, and the light vehicle went rattling forward 'neath the low-pitched portal of the town, into the open beyond.

With a litheness that lent his movements somewhat the supple swing of the panther, the man bent forward from the seat of the car, and with parted lips inhaled the

brisk air of morning that came wafted
towards them in long-drawn sweet-scented
breezes. Moist and cool came the wind,
for it was blown from across the Eubœan
Sea, that in long-swept waves flowed to
the right of their way, and with the briny
breath there came blended the quickening
scent from the olive groves aflower, which,
flanking the road on either side, and north-
wards, far as the eye could reach, clad
the Bœotian hills with green abundance.

" Look yonder, Mnemarchos ! " cried
the man with the dark flowing locks,
pointing athwart the sea, where, behind
the vanishing coasts of Eubœa, the early
rays of the sun, like the crested points
of some mighty diadem, were flashing forth,
— " look how Helios greets his well-
beloved Attika ! And how the waves, like
a mighty army, rank after rank, go surging
onward, panoplied in helmet and shield
of silver ; and lo, to the left, Parnassus
and Kithæron, bearing aloft their rugged
peaks ; and fronting us, the silver-flowing

Asopus. Gaze upon it all,—breathe, drink
deep of it. It is freedom, beauty, and all
combined,—this glorious Hellas."

In the dark eyes of the man there
burned a consuming fire ; more frequent
fell the blows on the horses' flanks, so
that at last they dashed into headlong
gallop, and with hoarse, broken yells he
inspirited them to ever wilder pace. At
length his gaze rested on his companion,
and, while bursting into ringing laughter,
he now checked the steeds into quieter
pace.

With cloak drawn under his chin, and
with a look of worried annoyance, Mnemarchos sat there silent and pallid.
" Fool that I was ! " he exclaimed, " to
forget that to journey with Praxiteles the
sculptor means surrendering one's self un-
conditionally into the grasp of a raving
madman ; well is it known that you artists
are friends of the gods and foes to man.
Your senses are all aglow, but your
hearts are ice."

"Right you may be," said Praxiteles, as a peculiar twitching flitted over his features.

"I know I am right," replied the other. "But still I do not know, even now, for what reason I am undertaking this break-neck drive with you."

"My eyes are athirst," rejoined the sculptor, "yearning for fresh forms."

"His eyes thirsting again!" said Mnemarchos, shrugging his shoulders; "when *will* they have drunk their fill?"

"You are aware of the fact," put in Praxiteles, "that the Sikyonians have vowed to Zeus in Olympia a statue of Hermes, and have commissioned me to——"

Now it was Mnemarchos' turn to laugh.

"And on that ground," he cried, "a reckless journey to Tanagra! Therefore must I drink disgusting sour country wine, cram myself with unsalted goat cheese, that Praxiteles may hunt up a model for his Olympian Hermes, 'mid the smooth-headed, full-stomached Bœotian peasants!"

" Maybe," returned the other, " I am urged
on by a right instinct. The Tanagrians, you
must know, celebrate to-day the feast of
Hermes, who is said to have freed of
yore the town of Tanagra from a dire
plague, by bearing a ram in procession
round the walls of the town."

" Had Hermes nothing better to do
than to preserve the stupid town ? "
muttered the other.

" The citizens assemble before the gates ;
the most beauteous youth in the town
plays the part of the god, bearing the
ram on his shoulders around the walls,
after which the animal is slain in festive
sacrifice."

" I begin to understand," replied Mnemarch. " O thou sculptor of my heart,
Praxiteles, thy friendship is the glory of
my life ; but the gods know such renown
has to be dearly bought."

As these words escaped his lips, the
chariot rolled along from out the dense
olive grove into the open landscape, and,

—" Tanagra ! " exclaimed both the travellers at one breath.

Hot and glaring shone the morning sun on the white walls of the town, crowning the summit of a tolerably high hill, which, fronting the two Athenians, rose sheer, and up whose slopes the roadway went circling. The festival seemed already in full swing, for on the topmost slope of the hill, encamped in densely-thronging groups, were people, clad in motley garments, that gave a lively aspect to the colourless chalk cliffs. Again the goad had to do its duty, and fast as the steep road would allow, the horses clambered up the path, crowned on all sides with vineyards. Scarce had they reached the topmost level, when, with dinning noise, and shouting, and jingling, the festive procession came moving onward straight towards them. It was headed by flute players, whose monotonous solemn tone gave the rhythm for those moving in procession ; next followed the controllers of the feast, who kept back the surging

crowd, and, when these had passed, there
rang out the unanimous wild cry of joy:
" Hail, Hermes of Tanagra ; Hail, fair
Myrtolaos! " At the same instant the
whole mass of beholders swayed towards
him to whom this acclamation was addressed ; and surrounded, nay almost borne
forward, by the throng of people, a fair,
blooming, tall, and slenderly-built youth
came treading along the path. The light
garment, held fast to the left shoulder by
a clasp, allowed free play to the right arm,
with which he held on his shoulder a snow-
white ram, with fore and hind legs bound
together, while in his left hand he bore
the attribute of the god, the Hermes staff.
With ease and freedom he moved on
beneath the ponderous weight of the
animal, his head poised backwards, so that
the dark curls, held together above his
forehead by a golden fillet, flowed down
his neck ; and as thus, glancing neither to
the right nor left, but with eyes looking
in dreamy unconsciousness into the azure

heavens, he passed by the strangers, he
afforded a sight as new as it was graceful.
Scarcely had they time, however, to take
in the impression of the quickly-passing
scene, when the pressig forward of the
throng told that the feast was not yet at
an end. With one quick strain at the
reins Praxiteles turned the horses round
in the direction of those that had preceded,
and keeping from the throng of people on
foot, he, in a quick trot, rounded the next
corner of the projecting town-wall. In the
open space, now in view, it was clear that
the chief and final act of the festival was
to be played. The middle of the space
was taken up by a mighty boulder of
rock, up which a few flat steps led, and
round which were ranged stone seats whereon
the ancient and venerated men of the town
seated themselves in contemplative repose.
This space was usually employed for the
popular meetings of the Tanagrians; to-day,
however, it had to serve other purposes, for,
instead of the orator who, with eyes severe,

had ruled the mob below, moving their
hearts at sound of his voice, there now
stood on the rock, with head modestly
bent, a female form, youthful and delicate.
She was clad in the picturesque style of
the Theban women ; from the uncovered
shoulders there flowed a long, white robe,
ending in a kind of train ; the dark-brown
hair was gathered above the parting into
a becoming knot, and from out sandals
of fine red leather peeped dainty white
feet. In her hands she bore a golden
bowl, heaped up with luscious strawberries.

" What is the meaning of this, and who
is the maiden ? " Mnemarch inquired of a
Tanagrian standing by.

" Thou art a stranger here," replied the
latter, " else wouldst thou know that,
after Hermes had carried the ram around
the town-walls, he was refreshed with
strawberries by the women of Tanagra.
In remembrance thereof, year by year, the
most beauteous of our maidens is chosen,

to feed the Hermes-youth with the hallowed fruit."

" And who is this most beauteous of your damsels ? "·

" Hellanodike, daughter of the rich Myronides, whom thou seest seated yonder."

Hermes - Myrtolaos had meantime reached the foot of the stone steps ; he threw the ram from his shoulders, which was at once seized by the controllers of the feast and borne to the sacrifice, while he mounted the first step. The girl let her eyes rest on him, and a deep roseate blush flushed her sweet face and in a crimson wave flowed over neck and shoulders, as the youth had reached the highest step, and stretched forth his hands towards the bowl she was holding.

" Nearer ! " cried Praxiteles to his com-panion, who had taken the reins in hand, as they had fallen from the grasp of the artist, rapt as he was in intense admiration.

" We can push no further with the

chariot," said Mnemarch, "the throng is too dense."

"Then stay by the chariot," was the other's reply ; and with a sudden leap he was in the midst of the crowd, through which he battled his way with arm and elbow till he reached the foot of the boulder.

There, at the top, they stood now close together, those two noble youthful forms ; and had two immortals lighted on earth they could not have looked other than these. The youth's forehead was aglow from the fatigue of the way, and his dark gleaming eyes rested in deep earnest dreaminess on the lovely features of the maiden, who was bending over him. A rapturous smile played around her lips as she did so, and her brow showed an expression of happily satisfied pride. Her lips moved softly, and the Athenian sculptor, who, with body leaning forward and with ardent glance, took in every trait, every glimpse of the charming picture, caught the words she whispered, " Hast thou discovered, Myrtolaos?" and in like manner his reply, "Not yet, Hellanodike."

For another moment the two stood, heedless of the surrounding crowd, solely wrapped in each other; then from the multitude, which began to be impatient, there arose shouts.

"Give food to Hermes, Hellanodike!" came the cry from one side; "Eat, Hermes!" from another. Those to whom the cries were addressed started from their reveries; Myrtolaos dipped his hand into the bowl, and lifted a couple of strawberries to his lips. Then, taking the vessel from Hellanodike's hands, he descended the steps, to distribute the contents to those standing by; for the custom of the feast ordained this, because to the fruit popular belief assigned some special virtue of healing. One of the first he encountered was the Athenian, with eyes dreamily drooped towards the ground; he tendered the bowl to the sculptor, when he felt it held fast, and at the same

moment heard a whispered voice, "I greet
thee, Hermes." He started, and on the
instant an indescribable feeling pervaded
him ; he felt himself straightway under
the secret sway of a strange powerful
influence, quickened by the fire of the
flashing eyes, which like two thirsty suns
seemed to sink into and absorb his whole
being. For a brief moment the fair
Tanagrian gazed speechless at the wonderful stranger; then his lips parted, as though
he would utter a sound, pronounce a
word ; yet ere he was able, the wave of
the thronging crowd had seized him, and
swept him away. Praxiteles gazed after
him. Once more Myrtolaos appeared
above the surging mass, once more he
turned his head, yet once more the eyes
of both met ; and then the waves swelled
over and around him. When the sculptor
looked round towards where Hellanodike
had stood, she had already left her post;
the Hermes feast was at an end.

In the house of the wealthy Myronides of

Tanagra a domestic household festival was evidently to be combined with the public ceremonial. Slaves were busied in fastening wreaths and festoons on the pillars and cornices of the fore-court, and the din caused by their laughing and chattering was so great that they were unaware of a chariot drawing up before the gate, and an impatient voice inquiring for Myronides, master of the house. These were the travellers from Athens, whose arrival was now announced to the owner, abiding in the inner court. As the latter, a man of noble bearing, with flowing grey hair and beard, appeared on the threshold, the Athenians went forward with gracious mien to meet him, and Praxiteles tendered him one half of a golden ring.

"I greet thee, Myronides," he said at the same time ; "Dexippos sends thee this from Athens."

With quick, keen glance Myronides examined the presented token, and thereupon said,—

"And whom do I greet in your persons, ye strangers twain?"

"This," said the sculptor, "is Mnemarchos, from Athens, and I am Praxiteles."

"What, Praxiteles the sculptor?"

"The sculptor."

"Then great good betide Dexippos," Myronides exclaimed, as he seized both hands of the Athenian, "for having vouchsafed me the honour to shelter the star of Attica. Enter, honoured guests, and be it known that in a happy moment are you come. I await some few friends to dinner, that they may while away with me the day that has brought joy to our town and honour to my house."

"By making thy fair child Hellanodike queen of to-day's Hermes festival?" asked Mnemarchos.

"And ye already know of it?" returned the master of the house, with contented smile. "Come! a bath after the tiring drive

will refresh you, after which you will find
us in the banqueting hall."

The spacious room into which the Athenians were led, after the heat and fatigue of the
journey had been calmed down, was decked
in festive guise, the guests had assembled, and
some were already reclining on couches ranged
round the table. But as soon as the name
" Praxiteles " was uttered, all present started,
all rose up, and thronged round the illustrious
man. But from a distant corner of the hall
two dark eyes, with wondering gaze, rested
on the bearer of that name. Praxiteles felt
thrilled by the glance, and, looking up, recognised Myrtolaos. Through the midst of the
other guests he went straight towards him,
grasped the blushing youth by both hands,
and said,—

" Hermes of Tanagra, thou who shalt once
live with Olympic Zeus, anew I greet thee."

Hearing the strange address, the guests
looked inquiringly at one another; yet, ere
they had time to exchange thoughts in whis-
pers, at a sign from the host slaves appeared,

bearing on silver staves wreaths of roses, white and red, which they placed on the brows of each respective guest. One was just nearing the Athenian master, when Myrtolaos, who up to then had been struggling with his shyness, suddenly sprang forward, and, having scrutinized Praxiteles for a brief moment with keen glance, selected a wreath of crimson-red full-blown roses, with which he approached him.

" Blessed be my hands," he said, with trembling voice, yet all so gently, as though he wished to prevent his words from reaching the rest ; " blessed that they may crown thee, great and noble Praxiteles ! " With these words he placed the wreath around his brow, and the Athenian felt how the youth's hands were trembling. He would have answered, but as he gazed in the large dark eyes, uplifted towards him, beaming with admiration, and yet seeming to dwell in the realm of their own dreamings, he remained silent, and let the youth silently do his office. Myrtolaos stepped back modestly, and, as the guests took their seats at the board, he sought his place at the lower end of the table.

The repast was bountiful and long drawn out. At length it came to an end, and in large stone jars the wine was served for dessert. Myrtolaos arose and left the hall, leaving the men to their converse.

As soon as he had left, Praxiteles turned towards the host.

" Tell me," he began, " Myronides, thou truly enriched, have these two young roses sprung up in thy garden ? Are they both thy children ? "

" I regard both as such," returned the Tanagrian, " although Hellanodike alone is of my own flesh and blood."

" And who and whence this youth, whom I admired at the Hermes' festival, and have found again in thy dwelling ? "

" Ten years have now elapsed," said Myronides, " since an old man, coming from the north, appeared in our town, in whose company was a remarkably handsome boy. The old man, tired out by long and

wearisome wandering, broke down; and as
this happened just before my threshold, I
took him into my house and nursed him in
his last flitting hours. When he saw death
was at hand, he summoned me to his couch;
the lad sat beside him, and with unceasing
tenderness the withered hand of the dying
man fondled the boy's dark curls.

" ' Leave me, Myrtolaos, my darling boy,
for a few moments,' he said to him ;—alas !
he never saw him more.

" ' I am dying,' he then murmured, turning
to me, ' and can leave thee nought in return
for thy generous dealing, for even as a beggar
did I enter thy dwelling ; but one treasure
I do possess, and willingly do I consign it to
thy keeping, for truly I look upon thee as a
worthy man, one of right noble character : it
is that child. Believe me, there is something
akin to the marvellous about him. I am
from Lokris, but Athens was his birthplace,
whence his parents had fled with him when
the thirty tyrants were ruling there. I
gave his father work, and the family lived

in a hovel that was in the field ; a wretched
abode it was, but I was poor and had
nothing better. The father died ; and the
woman, too weak to work, became a burthen
on my hands. But little heed was I taking
about her, when one night there came to me
a wonderful dream : I beheld the interior of
the shed, and in the centre stood a noble
statue in marble, covered with dust. The
eyes of the figure were fixed on me, its lips
opened, and with solemn, mournful tone it
said :

" " " Dost thou thus allow the treasure to
lie neglected that thy house possesses ? "

" ' I awoke ; and as soon as day dawned,
hastening to the hut they inhabited, I found
the widow stretched dead on her bed, and the
lad standing by her side. As I entered the
boy turned and gazed at me ; and in that
hour I resolved never to abandon him.
Thou hast heard,' the old man continued,
' that in times of old the Olympian gods are
believed to have descended to earth ; thou
dost regard it as a legend—even so did I. But

at that moment I saw it was possible, for before
me there stood in living embodiment one of
the inhabitants of Olympus— not mirthful, nor
joyous, as we picture to ourselves the dwellers
in eternal bliss; but a dreamy, young god,
whose brow betrayed the pain caused by his
exile amid the sorrows of mankind.'

" '" Myrtolaos," said I, and it seemed to
me as though I were touching what was
hallowed, as I laid my hand on his youthful
head, "wouldst thou remain with me, and
take me as thy father?"

" ' He raised his eyes to me, then nodding
his head without forwardness or shyness, he
seized my right hand. I threw my mantle
about him, for it was wintry weather, and
winters in the Lokrian mountains, as thou
knowest, are bitterly cold, and, pressing him
to my bosom, led him along the road to
my home, where I had neither kith nor kin.
" Behold this house," I said to him on entering;
" here shalt thou dwell as long as it please thee,
and thou shalt know it is truly thine own."
He then twined his arms about my neck,

and two large tear-drops trickled silently
down the noble features, his fair countenance
the while remaining undisfigured by the pangs
of sorrow beating through his breast. I got
ready a couch for him, for he was battling
against weariness, and his pillow I made as
soft as I was well able, wrapping him up
snugly in sheltering coverlets. Then when
he had fallen asleep, I stood for a long time
before him, marvelling over the human
destiny that had snatched this noble flower
from its native soil, that it might take root
again in my far-off humble abode. For
five long years,' the old man continued, ' we
have now lived together, during which
period there was not a moment wherein he
caused me sorrow. He gave me aid in all
the avocations of daily life, was my helpmate
at home and afield, and gladdened me by all
those unconscious yet all so kindly signs of
affection a noble human heart well knows how
to bestow. He awakened but one anxiety in
me : he was not happy, and the look of sadness would not quit his eyes. I marked well

that he led a twofold life ; for ever when the
day's labour was over, he would shrink into
solitude, and remain alone for hours at a
stretch. I did not disturb him, but once I
followed, and watching him unawares discovered him on a projecting cliff of the
mountain which afforded a wide view south-
ward. There he sat, at first involved in
dreaminess ; after which he arose, and I saw
how with his hands from a pit near by
he took clay, laden with which he wended
back to his favourite nook.' "

Praxiteles, who had followed the narrator's
story with intense interest, started at these
words.

" Took clay ? " he inquired.

" So ran the old man's story, and thus he
continued :—' He began to play with the soft
material, pressing and kneading it together,
and I noticed that his eyes lost their dreaminess whilst thus busied, and assumed an
expression of most eager attention ; now and
again pausing he glanced up, as though he
sought to fix the lines of some model he

fain would imitate, then returned to his
occupation. He gazed at what his fingers
had moulded, shook his head as discon-
tented, and flung everything over the cliff
into the deep. Good care I took not to let
him know I had been watching ; but when
he came home, and had partaken of the
evening meal, I said tenderly : "Myrtolaos,
is it not so, thou art unhappy to have to
live with me ? " He gazed at me with earnest
eyes. "No," he said, " not unhappy, but I
yearn——" " Yearn ? And for what ? " " I
am not able to tell," he replied, " for I know
not how to describe it, but sometimes it rushes
through my heart ; then I seem to grow conscious, I feel as though a dream of long, long
ago had taken possession of me,—a dream
of things wonderful and strange. Men are
standing around me, women too, fair as my
eyes have never beheld, but they are, as I
deem, no real beings, for they stand there
ever silent, ever motionless." "Thou meanest statues," I said interrupting, "such as
sculptors fashion ? " His eyes brightened

with flashing light, and he came close to my
side. "Tell me, father, are there men who
can achieve such?" "Certainly," I answered,
"the great sculptors in Athens are renowned
for it." "Oh!" he cried, "then my presentiment hath not deluded me." "Wouldst
thou fain learn this art?" I asked. He
trembled from inner emotion, and so softly,
as though he were confiding to me some
hallowed secret, he said: "Yea, father,
I believe I should like it right well. For
when that dream comes, seest thou, then the
forms array themselves around; I see them
quite near, quite clearly, and then a something
seizes me—I know not what; it lies cumber-
ing my breast, till I essay to recast their
shapes." "In kneaded clay?" I interrupted.
"Aye, aye!" he cried, utterly forgetting
himself, "dost thou also know how it is
done? Hast thou also tried? Oh! is it
not rare and glorious when one feels the
clay under one's hands,—feels that one might
fashion men, living things, nay, the whole
world therefrom, did one but understand the

art.   O my father !" and he suddenly clasped
my knees, " teach me this art!   Wilt thou?
I entreat thee, teach me ! "   I could not
refrain from smiling,' the old man continued,
' albeit I was in a most earnest mood.   " This
art," said I, "I am unable to teach thee."
He gazed at me bewildered ; and with an
expression, as though he could not grasp
why I could not fulfil his heart's yearning——' "

"It shall be fulfilled," suddenly broke
forth Praxiteles, who with heaving breast
had been earnestly following the story of the
narrator.   " And he who will teach him is
here present."   Springing from his seat he
strode up and down the hall, his large eyes
glowing like fire, and his heart throbbing
loudly within his breast.

"Summon the youth hither, Myronides,"
said he, turning towards him.   " I will
announce to him that Praxiteles himself will
teach him the hallowed art so much longed
for."

The aspect of the deeply-moved man,

his impassioned words, acted like magic on the surrounding guests. They sprang up one and all, crowding round Myronides and the Athenian artist, and murmured sounds of congratulation were heard from those present. One guest only stood apart, keenly observing the course of things. It was a young man of unprepossessing countenance, who, during the whole repast, had remained silent and reserved.

" Let me finish my story," Myronides said, smiling. Praxiteles, however, interrupted him with impatience.

" What further is there left to recount? The future is everything. The old man of whom you have told was with him on the journey to Athens, was he not? but on the way death overtook him ? "

" Thou hast guessed aright," replied the host.

" Praise be to his memory!" exclaimed the sculptor, " that he understood the voice of the gods; and praise to thee, Myronides, that thou didst receive the boy under thy hospitable roof; but henceforth," and the voice of the artist grew slow and solemn, "he does not any more belong to thee; to thee he did belong, henceforth he is mine and the gods'." There was something imposing in the gesture accompanying these words. The words themselves, outburst of a powerful nature, conveyed the victorious impress of earnest thought, so that they overpowered all who heard. Myronides, however, stood a brief moment sunk in thought. Now advanced the silent guest to the host, and taking him apart said softly, but impressively :—

"Why dost thou hesitate? Is not this the way most helpful to all?"

Myronides scrutinised him keenly.

"Certainly, as far as concerns thee, Phyallas," said he, in just as low a tone.

"And not for thee, equally?" answered the other sharply, "and for Hellanodike, thy daughter?"

Without answering ever a word Myronides drooped his head, and went straight up to Praxiteles.

"Thou requirest much of me, Praxiteles," said he, and his voice trembled somewhat. "It is hard for me to part with him; he has grown dear to my heart. He has taken root in this home, and if thou dost pluck him forth the earth will remain clinging to the roots, and more than one will feel it deeply. For even if he be not himself a god, yet is he of their chosen ones, and they gave him the gift they bestow on all their favourites,— the unseen charm to be beloved by men. Nay," said he, as Praxiteles would fain have interrupted, "I know what thou wouldst say, and feel that I must not cross his destiny. Yet forgive the question of a man riper in years than thou, Praxiteles; wilt thou make him happy?"

"Yea!" cried the Athenian, with solemnly uplifted hand, "if he be what I believe him to be, I shall make him happy."

"Thou sayest so," replied the other, "because thou art Praxiteles, the great master whom the gods have blessed; but

what knowest thou of him? Some words
uttered by a crazed old man afford the
sole warrant that he doth possess what
alone may render the artist's life endur-
able,—true genius."

Praxiteles looked at him in deep emotion.

"Thou claimest too much, Myronides,"
he said; "can I say more than this, I
believe in him? believe in the feeling
that took hold of me when first to-day
I looked into his dark dreamy eyes;
believe in him since learning the story
of his childhood."

"Well then," returned Myronides, "I
will bring him to thee, and he shall himself
decide as to his lot."

Myronides left the apartment with his
other guests; Praxiteles remained alone,
absorbed in deep thought; he paced up
and down while slaves, by the light of
torches, were clearing away the fragments
of the feast.

"Come hither," said Praxiteles, when
the last of them was about to quit the

apartment. " Is there any clay to be had
in this house ? "

" Clay ? "

" Aye, clay, potter's clay."

As chance would have it, a heap of clay
was lying in the courtyard, and Praxiteles
ordered the slave to bring him a platterful.
In wonderment he obeyed ; when brought,
the sculptor made sign to the slave to withdraw, threw off his upper garment, and
in flurried haste, with both hands clutched
the soft material, which he kneaded and
deftly moulded, keeping his eyes the while
looking into space, as if they sought to
fix the object his hands were modelling ;
and whilst working with wonderful deftness
there grew beneath his hands the shape
of a human head. Quite absorbed in his
work, with twitching lips and flashing
eyes, he kept on without break till he
had advanced so far as to be able to set
the model on the table, after joining a
neck to the life-sized head. At that
moment Myronides with Myrtolaos and

Mnemarch returned; behind them came Phyallas. In suspended wonder they remained standing, for the first object meeting their eyes, illumined by the flickering torchlight, was the work of Praxiteles. Myrtolaos uttered a startled cry, rushed close up to the table, whereon the sculptor had set his work, and stood with heaving breast, silent and transfixed.

In spite of the haste with which it was fashioned the head was indeed of fascinating beauty. The Hermes was represented with head gently inclining, and the features recalled by their rapt expression the Hermes of Tanagra.

Praxiteles stood near the table, and with scrutinising glance gazed at the youth, who had time to recover from his wonderment. Then he turned laughingly towards the others.

" I have been diverting myself while you were away," he said, and he made a movement as though he would destroy what he had been shaping. On the instant

Myrtolaos rushed towards him, exclaiming in pleading tones,—" Do not destroy, oh, do not destroy it ! " The eyes of the Athenian flashed with unwonted fire.

" Myrtolaos," he murmured in a low voice, " wouldst thou too like to create such things ? "

The youth looked at him, unable to find utterance.

" Wilt thou learn it, Myrtolaos ? Wilt thou learn from the Athenian Praxiteles ? "

" Teach me thy art ! " entreated the youth, and as if seized by a supernatural power, he sank on his knees before the great master. " Teach me thy art, glorious, great Praxiteles ! "

" If thou wouldst become my pupil," said Praxiteles, " thou must follow me to Athens ; art thou prepared so to do ? "

" I am ready, let me follow thee whithersoever thou goest."

" Thou must quit this abode, Myronides thy father, all whomsoever thou hast cherished in this home ; wilt thou do so ? "

" I will," said Myrtolaos, as he gazed at the sculptor with flashing eyes.

" Well then," exclaimed Praxiteles, laying his hand on the youth's head, " then do I take possession of thee, Myrtolaos, and dedicate thee to the service of the gods, who have until now unawares to thee taken hold of thy heart ; I will unseal thine eyes, that thou mayst recognise the gods."

By no word had Myronides interrupted the solemn scene. Seeing all was now decided, he advanced to Myrtolaos, silently extending his arms, and the youth threw himself upon the breast of the worthy man.

" He is thine now," said Myronides to Praxiteles ; " take him with thee when thou wilt."

" To-morrow then," said the sculptor.

It had grown late ; the inmates of the house had retired to rest, Praxiteles also betook himself to his apartment.

Mnemarchos, however, ere following the example of the others, went into the garden

that stretched far behind the house. The
night was mild, but a soft breeze came wafted
over the distant sea from the south-east, cooling the sultry air, and bearing with it from
the landscape around the perfume of the olive
trees. From the garden, lying high above
the city, there was a far view into the blue
distance; the moon at full shone through the
calm air, irradiating with soft, silvery light
the barren mountain tops, while the olive
groves skirting them were wrapped in soft
shadows. It was not this lovely picture of
nature that filled the mind of the man who,
with fevered brow, was pacing up and down
the garden ; another picture, more striking,
stood before his mind's eye, and as it sunk
deeper and deeper into his fancied dreams,
made his blood seethe. He bethought him
of Hellanodike. From the moment he had
beheld her at the Hermes festival, her image
had not quitted his mind, and a wild desire
of possessing the beautiful, young, and blooming being was cherished in his mind.

Just as he reached the end of a dark-covered walk, he heard a sound of voices, and beheld before him, in the moonlight, two youthful figures with arms entwined; they were Myrtolaos and the daughter of Myronides. The Athenian sank back within the shadow of the trees.

"So, now thou hast found what thou wert yearning for, Myrtolaos?" said the young girl in earnest, well-nigh sorrowful tones to her companion.

"Yea, Hellanodike," answered the youth, "the presentiment that whispered I should some day realize the desire of my life has not deluded me. I have done so." Hellanodike gazed in silence into the dim beyond.

"Look, how Kithæron shimmers in the white moonlight," said she. "That is the gate of Attica; and behind, far, far behind, lies Athens, and there thou wilt dwell while I linger here."

A great sob burst from her bosom, and whilst her tear-drops fell fast, she threw her arms round the neck of the youth she loved, and their lips met in one long kiss.

Mnemarch pressed his forehead against the tree concealing him. He heard not the touching broken accents that came from the heart that was near to breaking with sorrow, for he was only moved by consuming passion. He only saw how the light garment fluttered back from the arms uplifted ; how the shining moon displayed the softness of their contour ; and beheld the loosened hair floating over the graceful neck. His longing grew into desire, and he began to revolve plans whereby he might gratify his passion.

"Myrtolaos," the girl sobbed in choking impassioned voice, "thou whose wishes were my wishes, in whose sorrow I sorrowed, must it be that thou leave me ? Must thou depart ? "

"Hellanodike," he tremblingly replied, pressing her closer to his breast, "why have the gods enjoined on me that I must make those whom I love and who love me unhappy by this mysterious prompting which urges me? Hellanodike, I cannot remain ; go I must to Athens with him,—I must !"

"Full well I know," she replied in sorrowful tones, "thou canst not live as others do here, else thou knowest the father had not refused thee his daughter ; but thou hast told me the narrow walls of Tanagra stifle thee, and therefore must thou away to glorious, dazzling Athens. There thou wilt live and work under sway of thy gods and goddesses, and companioned by them wilt forget all who think of thee here. And Hellanodike will now become the wife of Phayllas—of Phayllas," she exclaimed shuddering, and hid her face on the breast of her beloved.

In silent agony Myrtolaos stood by her side, unable to utter a word, for in his own soul there dawned, mayhap for the first time, a consciousness how much of beauty, love, and assured happiness he was surrendering for a dim, shadowy future ; and yet, whilst he felt the sweet loving heart beating against his breast, it seemed as if there floated from Attica towards him a procession of sublime beings, beckoning with serious looks as they whispered, "Thou belongest to us;" he

sank in silence, and could not say, "Hellanodike, I will stay here."

At that moment was heard a rustling in
the bushes, and the two lovers, startled by
the noise, were joined by a third. It was
Mnemarchos.

"Be not fearful," he said, "it is a friend
who comes. Do ye not recognise me?"

"Mnemarchos the Athenian," said Myrtolaos, "the friend of Praxiteles."

"And thy friend," replied he, "who comes
to announce that you sorrow needlessly, for
the wishes of both shall be fulfilled, and yet
ye shall remain unsevered."

Hellanodike, with her large guileless eyes,
gazed at him bewildered.

"What meanest thou, strange man?" she
said, with trepidation.

"I mean," replied Mnemarch, "that
Phayllas, whom thou lovest not, shall not be
thy husband; that thou shalt go forth from
here away to Athens."

She shuddered. "But my father?" she
said, shyly.

"What I propose," said the Athenian, "will, of course, at first cause sorrow to thy father ; for as he would not yield assent to thy wishes, it must happen without his knowledge. He is a noble man, and a friend of art, and hereon I build my plan. When Myrtolaos becomes an artist and sculptor, as we hope—and from the studio of Praxiteles there have gone forth no mere dabblers,—when he has achieved his first great work, then will he appear with thee in thy father's presence, will lay his work at his feet, and will say, 'I did thee wrong, Myronides, but. I did so because I could not separate from my art nor from Hellanodike, thy child, and here is the price wherewith I fain would win back forgiveness and thy heart,' and Myronides will forgive both him and thee."

These words were uttered with such convincing eloquence, that the youthful listeners felt deeply moved thereby.

"O Hellanodike," whispered Myrtolaos, pressing her softly to his heart, "would thou hadst the courage !"

"She will have the courage," Mnemarch
answered in her stead, "if she loves truth,
and if she really wish thee to become an
artist; for only in presence of the beloved one
is the artist inspired to great works imbued
with life ; or do you believe Praxiteles and
the other great masters were able to do what
they have achieved without being inspired by
the presence of their beloved ones?"

Unwittingly he spoke these last words in a
cynical tone; the two pure young souls heard,
but understood him not.

"What a friend have the gods sent us in
this blessed hour !" exclaimed the youth.
"O Hellanodike, beloved one, his plan is
so beautiful and abounding in promise, say
that thou wilt."

She shuddered and trembled, and prompted
by a feeling unutterable, pressed closer to
him.

"But my father," she said softly, "will
seek for me, and find me."

Mnemarch appeared to reflect for a
while.

"For that also," said he, "care is taken.
I know one place where he will not seek
for thee; abide with me, in my house."

"In thy house?" and she unwittingly
drew back a step.

"Thou must not be filled with tremors,"
said he, in a persuasive voice; "I dwell
alone with my mother.   Thou shalt be under
her protecting care."

"Calm thy anxieties," exclaimed Myrtolaos,
who seemed to have awoke to new life.
"Dost thou not hear that this man really
is offering us counsel like a true friend?
Say that thou wilt go with us."

A secret conflict seemed to pervade her
soul, as she all-silently and with streaming
eyes looked back at her father's house.   Then
she spoke in clear, quiet tones,—

"Myrtolaos, I will."   And turning towards Mnemarch, she softly added, "And
now I put myself under thine and thy
mother's sheltering care until we return to
my father.   Is it not so, beloved?"

"Until we return to him," answered he,

joyously, and kissed the tears from her eyes.

The die was cast. It was decided not to make known as yet any of the plan to Praxiteles, but a time was fixed, ere many days were sped, when Hellanodike was to appear at the olive grove at the foot of the mountain. In that grove Mnemarch should await her with a chariot, and conduct her to Athens.

" O come thou also," said she to Myrtolaos, as she heard this last proposal, and her words betrayed alarm. Mnemarch bit his lips.

" He shall accompany me," said he quickly, " and thou shalt make the journey together with us both."

Then they separated, and Mnemarch sought his chamber.

As Hellanodike and Myrtolaos had timidly passed over the threshold, where no sound was to be heard, with a sudden movement the girl threw herself on her knees.

" Come," she said, and drew her beloved to her ; " it has so long been a kindly home

to us. We will pray to the gods, that it
may again receive us with open welcome."

Like to golden butterflies did the first
rays of the morning sun flutter into the
studio of Praxiteles at Athens. They hovered about, parted company, joined again, and
circled round, as if afraid of lighting on the
flowers of this garden, comprising works of
art, statues, and busts, which, finished or
half achieved, ranged along the walls or
lay scattered amongst the columns in wonderful profusion. At last one little sly sun-
beam took heart, and nestled in the midst
of a labyrinth of curls on the head of a
dreamily dainty young faun ; yet another
more courageous offspring of the sun, fastened
on the swelling lips of the beautiful Aphrodite ;
near by a third nestled close to the goddess,
with loving caresses loitering on her bosom.
And the lovely goddess felt the soft glow
of the endearment throughout her marble
limbs. She grew irradiated with a smile, and
the stony faces around took life from her

smile. A divine joyousness permeated the
noble hall. It seemed as though limbs were
moving, and arms were stretched out lovingly,
and as though the creations of Praxiteles were
greeting their own and their great framer's
heavenly parent,—the radiant young sun of
Athens.

Amid all these gladsome things stood
Myrtolaos, lost in rapt admiration. Thoughts
unspeakable pervaded his breast; the
dreams of his early days had assumed shape
and life ; but what he saw around was so
overpowering, seeming to him the impress
of a nature so high above his own, that
he felt it as one almost strange to him,
and a feeling of overwhelming wonder was
uppermost in his mind. More especially
was this so as he stood face to face
with a work of art that seemed but just
finished by the master, and which, somewhat apart from the rest, stood where steps
led from the studio to the artist's abode.
It represented Aphrodite descending to the
bath, and what no sculptor had heretofore

ventured on here stood achieved. The
goddess was unapparelled, unadorned, and the
female form stood revealed to the eye of
the beholder. What streams of glowing
inspiration must have quickened the breast,
that could conceive the idea of a being
bathed in the rays of beauty, and what
powerful self-mastery withal must have
dwelt in the mind, that had known how to
keep every glimpse of base feeling far re-
moved from this beautiful creation. Unconsciously he shook his head. It seemed to him
as if there arose before him an obstacle
insurmountable ; as if he were peering into
a land he was never destined to enter.

Suddenly a slight rustling startled him.
There fell at his feet a dark red full-blown
rose, which must have been thrown from
behind him, and as in wonder he bent to
lift it there rang out a clear silvery, roguish
laugh. He turned and gazed into the
beaming eyes of a charming woman, who, arm
in arm with Praxiteles, was standing on the
steps leading to the apartment' of the latter.

They must both have long been gazing
at the dreamer, for only in such wise
could one explain the roguish waywardness
with which the beautiful stranger somewhat boldly and searchingly scanned the
blushing Myrtolaos. But the countenance
of Praxiteles had also assumed an expression different from heretofore: the solemn
earnestness Myrtolaos had observed in
him at the house of Myronides had
vanished, and from his dark eyes there
flashed forth a warm and radiant glad-
someness.

With inimitable grace the lovely woman
threw her arm round the neck of the
sculptor, and nestling close to him, said :—

"O Praxiteles, much renowned, every day
brings fresh homage for thee; yet few
as I deem have been so intensely felt
as the silent one we have just witnessed
here.—Come hither, thou beautiful boy,"
said she, turning to Myrtolaos, stretching
out her hand to him as he shyly approached. As soon as he had touched

her hand, she retaining it firmly, leaned down from the steps and imprinted a hearty kiss on the handsome Tanagrian's lips. The latter displayed such a look of bewilderment that Praxiteles and his companion, in spite of themselves, broke into mirthful laughter.

"Fear not!" exclaimed the woman, "take no shame at being kissed by Phryne, the Aphrodite of Cnidos."

Myrtolaos turned and glanced at the statue, and then looked back with an exclamation of surprise—the original of the goddess was standing living before him.

"Dost thou recognise her?" cried Praxiteles with a joyous, triumphant smile. "And is she not worthy that the dwellers in Cnidos, among whom she is to abide in future, should look up to her, and say, 'She cometh from Olympus'?"

Phryne stopped the flow of his words by pressing her lips on his.

"Unhallowed Prometheus that thou

art!" she said, "who art able not only to fashion men, but even gods out of material so profane."

"Nay, say not so!" cried Myrtolaos suddenly; "do not term this frame that has been the model for such a master-piece, unholy." His eyes were replete with radiance, and as to a loftier being he glanced up to Praxiteles.

"How earnest his speech, and how earnest his look!" said Phryne. "The woman that will once be his beloved will have to be of different cast from thy Phryne, O Praxiteles, for he will reverence her, and from her expect that she be adorable. But how?" she interrupted herself, seeing that Myrtolaos coloured deeply; "mayhap the young butterfly has already found a flower in whose calyx he hath been en-trapped? Come, out with it, thou self-betrayer, for here stands Praxiteles, thy master,—from him thou durst not with-hold any secret."

Myrtolaos turned aside, an inexplicable

feeling stopped him from uttering Hellanodike's name in presence of Phryne.

At this moment the curtain dividing
the studio was drawn aside, and Mnemarch
entered with a greeting. He had, imme-
diately on laying aside his travelling dress,
resumed the habits of Athenian life, and
appeared in rather dandified guise, the
exaggerated youthfulness of his garb contrasting all the more with the faded look
of his features.

" Permit me to kiss thy foot, god-like
Phryne," said he, " since Praxiteles has
planted it already in Olympus, it is a pious
act to pay such homage."

" As I am aware how hard it is for
thee to bend, I take thee at thy word,"
said Phryne, laughing ; " there, kiss my
foot !" She drew back the hem of her
garment somewhat, and displayed the classic-
moulded bared foot. Mnemarch bent
down, and touched it slightly with his
lips.

" Well, Myrtolaos," turning to him,

"the day has arrived and Hellanodike awaits us ; art thou ready ? "

" What means this ? " said Praxiteles with inquiring glance, while Myrtolaos threw a look of reproach at the speaker.

" Oh, by the gods," said Mnemarch carelessly, " thou needst not blush, Tanagrian, that thou hast an artist's blood coursing through thy veins ; and Praxiteles will not chide on hearing that thou hast persuaded her to follow thee to Athens, so that thou mayst become a worthy pupil of thy master."

" And was Myronides aware of this ? " asked Praxiteles, gravely.

" He will learn it," cried Myrtolaos, " when I go to him with the first work I have achieved under thy eyes, Praxiteles."

" So, then, you have contrived all without his being aware. The love that inspires you both is deep and mighty then ? "

" Harken to him ! " said Phryne, laughingly ; " Praxiteles has taken his seat on the philosopher's chair. Oh, but that does not suit

thee ; thou shalt verily sculpt me as Pythia,
seated on the prophetic tripod, for I have
divined aright on looking into this one's face."
Her jest, however, found no echo, for Praxiteles
remained erious and absorbed in thought.

"Has she friends in Athens?" said he,
turning to Myrtolaos, "and where and with
whom would she abide?"

"At thy friend's, Mnemarchos," replied
the youth, shyly; "he hath kindly offered her
his abode as a dwelling-place."

Praxiteles gave an involuntary start, and
there was a deep fold showing between his
brows. He seemed about to speak; Mnemarch
had turned aside with seeming indifference and
was busied in examining a satyr which seemed
to engage his whole attention ; Praxiteles
remained silent. In strange excitement he
paced up and down the studio; then he approached Mnemarch. The two conversed in
low but earnest tones. Through Mnemarch's
persuasive words the stern expression of
Praxiteles' face relaxed, and at last he advanced to Myrtolaos smiling as before.

" Thou hast begun thy new career with a daring exploit," he said ; " and Myronides' ire shall not be directed against me, for I knew nothing of this project; but forsooth, if she hath decided to follow thee of her own free choice, I will not thwart you ; show now thou art a true artist, for what we admire in a noble steed, we punish in the humdrum nag."

" Well spoken," cried Phryne ; " and rightly done. Tanagrian, here ! bear this ornament from Phryne's arm to Hellanodike, thy beloved ; let it be a pass-token when she comes to enter at the gates where dwell the gods ! "

" They dwell in Athens," cried Myrtolaos ; and at the sight of the glorious woman, who had detached a massive gold armlet, letting it slip into his uplifted hand, a feeling of living joyousness heretofore unknown came over him. Like a flash of lightning it pierced his very soul, and with a fire that quickened his whole being. To him it seemed as though only now were his eyes opened to the grandeur of the works of the master to whom he had vowed homage.

"Give me strength, ye gods," he cried, uplifting his arms; "let this glow now pervading me, remain at full within me, then, O Praxiteles, I shall some time strive against even thee."

"Come, come, enthusiast," said Mnemarch; and, as if rapt in ecstasy, Myrtolaos went forth with him.

Two days later a travelling-car set down its occupants before Mnemarchos' house; the master of the mansion, Myrtolaos, and a third, who, with timid beating heart, crossed over the threshold,—Hellanodike.

How bitter the hours since, with consciousness of the deceit practised, she dressed herself as for a harmless saunter; the tears she had to keep from bursting forth well-nigh burdened her heart as she quitted her father's abode, and now, perhaps for the last time, she wended her way down the well-known mountain path; but her courage remained unflinching amid her sufferings; she had promised to come, and she came.

In the dark olive-grove at the foot of the

mountain the chariot awaited, as arranged,
and Mnemarch, who saw her coming from
afar, hastened forth to meet her. A shudder
passed through her every limb on perceiving
him ; silently she rejected the proffered hand,
and her beating heart only then grew quieter,
when she recognised Myrtolaos, who had
remained by the chariot, and held the horses
by the reins.

In her long garment, flowing down to her
feet, which in soft folds clung around the
graceful contours of her body, her head
covered by a low-crowned hat, affording
a deep shade to her features, slowly she
advanced from between the trees. To the
youth it seemed as though he saw her for the
first time ; and, in truth, he beheld her for the
first time beside another, for in his thought
Phryne's image appeared by Hellanodike's
side. How beautiful were both, yet what a
contrast !

All silent was the meeting; for Myrtolaos
knew full well by the tear-veiled eyes that
she was too overcome with emotion to find

utterance ; moreover, silence and caution were enjoined. Mnemarch snatched the reins, and with flurried haste, as though it depended on him to convey away a stolen treasure in safety, he goaded the steeds on to the swiftest of their pace.

The drive was rapid and in silence. What words could she utter, as the rolling wheels said loud enough that one mile after the other was being placed between her and him who would at eve be awaiting her in anguish, —Myronides, her father.

At last Athens was reached, and the noisy throngs of people in the streets, the splendour of the public buildings, the glory of magnificence such as they had never before beheld, which now on all sides presented itself to their wondering eyes, exercised an influence overpowering on the daughter of quiet Tanagra. She drew near to Myrtolaos.

"I am all in trepidation," she softly said ; "methought Athens was a different town to ours ; but it is quite another world."

The house into which Mnemarchos led his

guest was spacious, and showed the wealth of the possessor. As soon as they entered, an old crone came forth from the inner court to meet them, who coaxingly seized Hellanodike's hands, pressed her to her heart, and eagerly inquired after the well-being of the "sweet dove," as, with assumed tenderness, she styled Hellanodike.

"Now, mother," said Mnemarch aloud, "is all in readiness even as I enjoined? hast thou decked the women's apartments in fit manner for our gracious visitor?"

At the word "mother" her wrinkled features assumed a fiendish grin, which at once vanished at a threatening glance from Mnemarchos.

"All is cared for," said she, "so as to content the 'sweet dove;' everything will gratify her, Mnemarchos, and she will say that old Timoessa well knows what sweet young hearts desire."

She chuckled, and Hellanodike involuntarily withdrew her hands from the bony fingers that grasped them like the claws of an owl.

If Mnemarchos had been unsympathetic to
her, his mother seemed even more irksome.

" The night draws on," said Mnemarchos,
" and Hellanodike will need rest ; we will
consign her to my mother's care, and ask her
to-morrow how she spent her first night in
Athens." With these words he sought to
induce Myrtolaos to depart with him ; but
Hellanodike held the latter fast by the hand.

" Abide with me still," she said, and her
look, brimful of solicitude, was fixed on
him.

" He shall stay as long as thou wishest,"
replied Mnemarchos; " only be mindful that
my mother is a strict guardian." He made
a sign to the old woman, and they left the
room together.

" Take good care," he said to her, when
outside, " he does not remain too long, and
meantime watch them closely ; thou art to
repeat to me every word they say."

She rubbed her hands.

" Why, thou talkest as though I were
a silly thing without experience, and knew

nothing of the nooks and crannies of the house, which afford scope for two attentive ears."

"And then again," he said harshly, "keep thy features better under restraint ! Thou didst laugh erewhile when I called thee ' mother.' "

"One is not used to the honour of it yet," she returned, with a hideous chuckle.

As soon as Hellanodike found herself alone with her beloved, her long upheld strength forsook her, and she burst into a flood of tears.

"Things are not as they should be in this house," she sobbed, "and it will bring no blessing to us if I abide here ! In the faces of these people, in the very air I breathe here, there is something which fills me with dread, and which I am unable to fend off." She had joined her arms about his neck, and gazed at him like to a gazelle tracked by a panther.

"This fear comes from the novelty of the surroundings," Myrtolaos replied, soothingly.

"Are not these people friendly and kindly disposed towards thee? Thou wilt soon find thyself at home here, Hellanodike, as I have done already."

She looked at him inquiringly.

"Hast thou found thyself at home here, Myrtolaos?"

"Yea," he exclaimed, and before his mind's eye Phryne's laughing lips appeared; "and that thou mayst see thou art awaited here with friendly feeling, receive this," and he proffered Phryne's golden armlet.

"Who sends me this?" she said, in astonishment.

"Phryne, friend of Praxiteles."

She tried the ornament round her arm.

"It is too wide," she said, smiling sadly, "and does not suit me."

It was as she said; the difference between the delicate proportions of the young maiden and the full-grown development of the woman was too marked.

"Then keep it as a gift," said Myrtolaos, "for as such was it given me."

She retained the golden ornament thoughtfully in her hands.

"Friend of Praxiteles?" she asked; "how do you understand that, Myrtolaos?"

He did not know what to answer, and remained silent.

"Are they man and wife?"

"Nay," he answered, abruptly.

"But they will become so?"

"I know not," said he, "but believe not."

She regarded him silently, all bewildered.

"The lady-friends of the artists," said he, blushing, "are united by spiritual bonds; they co-operate in their works, inspire their thoughts, and quicken their eyes that crave after beauty."

She smiled.

"Then the women of whom thou speakest must be beautiful?"

He encircled her slender form, drew her towards him, and kissed her.

"And art thou not beautiful, Hellanodike?" exclaimed he. Her cheek lay against his, and her lips were close to his ear.

"Myrtolaos," she whispered, and it seemed as if she were afraid of him, as if in the kiss he had given there were a strange fervour, "I should not like to be thy friend."

He stepped back.

"Then thou wouldst not have me an artist, renowned throughout Greece?"

She regarded him with silent reproof, and the whole fervour of his love came over him.

"Not my friend shalt thou be," he murmured; "my beloved thou art, and my wife shalt thou become."

The former sweet, childlike smile came anew to her countenance, and she allowed him once more to press her to his heart, and kiss her before he took leave. Then he left her. At that moment Timoessa appeared, to lead her to the women's quarters prepared for her.

These ranged round a square courtyard, which was converted into a garden, in whose midst, springing forth from an artificial rock, one heard the rhythmic and melodious plash of a fountain. An open passage, supported

by gaily-coloured pillars, ran around, and
formed the forecourt to the apartments, which
could be shut off by light rush matting from
the court, which gave them light and air. In
the warm season, however, now prevailing,
they stood open, and from one of the cham-
bers there gleamed a soft, subdued light,
coming from the sconce hanging from the
ceiling. On the threshold there stood a
slender young girl, who with large, peering
eyes awaited her coming.

" Up, Chlenusa," the old woman cried ;
" here is thy new mistress ; have good care
of her, for it will be thy duty to make her
feel at home here. Hast thou prepared the
couch ? "

The girl pointed silently towards
the chamber. By the light of the lamp,
one perceived that it was furnished with
every luxury which could then be pro-
cured ; in the middle stood the couch,
decked with white linen and light coverings.

Timoessa went out, and Hellanodike

seated herself upon the couch, dreamily looking out into the dark garden, and breathing in the sweet air which came wafted therefrom.

Chlenusa, with her flashing black eyes, was leaning against the door, gazing at her.

" Shall I sing to thee ? " asked she, without altering her position. " Many beautiful songs I know." Hellanodike turned her glances upon her. " Or shall I read thy hand ? " she exclaimed, and with sudden gesture she knelt down at the feet of Hellanodike. The latter caressingly stroked her soft black hair.

" Dost thou understand such art ? " asked she.

" I understand it well ; I can divine thy good fortune in thy hand, and would fain announce it."

Hellanodike smiled doubtingly.

" Good fortune ? Dost thou believe in it ? Wouldst thou wish it ? "

" Verily I do, because thou art so fair,"

answered the girl, whose eyes glittered like
diamonds. "The beautiful are happy in
Athens. One strews flowers in their path,
and riches and glory are theirs ; to them one
grants what one forbids to others ; the laws
yield to them, and even the judges themselves."

Hellanodike listened bewildered.

" Art thou an Athenian ? "

" I know not," replied the girl, and shook
her clustering curls, so that they fell in dark
shadows over her bronzed features ; "she
saith so, for she is from Athens, and calls
herself my mother ; but I place no belief
in her."

"In whom ? Of whom dost thou
speak ? " inquired Hellanodike.

" Be silent !" exclaimed Chlenusa, in sudden
terror, and pressed Hellanodike's knees
against her beating heart. " How beautiful
thou art," she exclaimed, " and how I love
thee ! O that I were so beautiful, only half
as charming, half as beautiful as thou ! "

" Thou strange one," replied Hellanodike,

5

who at this passionate strange homage blushed shyly.

" There are many beautiful women in Athens," she continued ; " but they all look down upon one, and therefore I hate them all,—I hate them ! " She sprang up, and her countenance as well as her words was replete with passion and hatred. " But thy eyes are so beautiful and so mild," and she knelt down again, " thou wilt not despise the brown Chlenusa, beautiful mistress ? Thou wilt not chide, if Chlenusa says she loves thee ? "

" I love all who love me," added Hellano-dike, " and I will believe that thou lovest me ; we shall be friends."

The girl sprang up, snatched up a tambourine standing in the corner of the chamber, and whilst she commenced a glad-some chant which exalted the god of love, Eros, to the accompanying sound of the jingling bells before the astonished eyes of Hellanodike, she began a wild dance, in which the lithesome figure developed a

wonderful play of limb. A demoniac passion burst from her, and she shook her
curling locks like a bacchante. Then she
hurled the instrument into the far corner,
and returned to her former post.

" Oh, how I will serve thee ! " said she,
still panting from the wild dance, " how I
will show thee all I know, all I can do.
Come, come, let me read and tell thee what
is written in thy hand ! " She seized anew
Hellanodike's hand, and the latter was unable to draw back from the strange being.

Chlenusa laid open the small white hand
which lay in her own fevered grasp, and bent
down low to peer at the lines in the palm.
She muttered to herself some disconnected,
hurried words, then looked upwards at Hellanodike.

" How wilt thou be famed above all
women of thy native town," said she in
almost reverent tone; " but thou art not
from Athens ? "

" That hast thou read in my hand ? "
asked Hellanodike.

The girl drooped her head.

"I do!" she continued slowly, "and how he loves thee!"

"Who?" cried Hellanodike, suddenly, "who is he of whom thou speakest? Who loves me?"

"Not one alone loves thee, there are many; but two stand foremost, they contend with each other for thee. Let me see"—and she bent down lower, and it was to Hellanodike as if the hand that held her own trembled—"let me see who will gain the victory."

Hellanodike snatched her hand away.

"Wilt thou read from my hand," she cried, "what stands written in my heart? Wilt thou prophesy what I have myself decided?"

The girl crouched on the ground, covering her face with her hand.

"Art thou angry with Chlenusa?" asked she, after a pause; and as her hands fell, her impassioned eyes had taken an expression of entreaty, and were bedewed with tears.

Hellanodike felt as though she were under the spell of this mysterious being.

"Canst thou name the two?" she asked hesitatingly. Again Chlenusa grasped her hand.

"I cannot find their names," she said, "but one is an artist—oh! what is that?" she interrupted herself abruptly. "Dost thou know Praxiteles?"

Hellanodike smiled despite the tremor that ran through her during this mysterious proceeding.

"Praxiteles, dost thou mean him?"

"No!" murmured she; "but it is so great an artist, that I fancied it must be the divine Praxiteles."

"O Myrtolaos," sighed Hellanodike in blissful self-forgetfulness, "and he loves me?" she murmured, as her sweet face turned towards the soothsayer at her feet.

Chlenusa did not look up.

"Yea! but one there is that loves thee still more."

"Does he dwell in my native town?" said

Hellanodike, in a low voice, bethinking her of Phayllas.

" No ; for Athens is not thy native town, and he lives in Athens."

The other grew more attentive.

" In Athens ? "

" Yes, yes ! I cannot further describe him ; but one thing I do perceive, thou art afraid of him, albeit he wishes thee well. He loves thee dearly, more earnestly, he is more faithful to thee than the other, for between him and thyself there stands a woman whose beauty has ensnared him."

Hellanodike's eyes began to flash—

" Another whom he loves more than me ? "

" Yea ! " said the girl, and her speech became more hasteful, " for she is a witch ; whoso has beheld her must fain be enticed by her beauty. Hast thou never heard of Phryne ? "

" Phryne, the friend of Praxiteles ? " almost screamed Hellanodike, bethinking her of the armlet Myrtolaos had brought her.

" It is so, it is so ! " whispered Chlenusa.

"But the other one only thinks of thee, longs for, cares for no other ; and if thou art responsive to his suit, thou wilt be famous, glorious, and happy."

"Avaunt ! thou bribed deceiver, in whom I foolishly reposed trust," cried Hellanodike, flushing out angrily. She tore her hand away from Chlenusa, and lifted her foot as if she would have spurned the girl away ; then she sank down on the couch and broke into tears. Suddenly she felt her feet clung to ; Chlenusa's burning lips covered them with passionate kisses, and she felt the girl's tear-drops raining down upon them.

"Weep not, sweet lady !" she stammered forth. "If Chlenusa has wounded thee, she will suffer for it; in thy hands is written happiness, and thou shalt live in peace and blissfulness."

She lay upon the ground quivering like to a beautiful wild creature. Hellanodike made sign to her silently to withdraw. Obediently she rose, and vanished into the gloom of the garden.

Sunk in sorrowful thoughts, Hellanodike remained alone.

What a dim foreboding had told her from the first was now made clear by the words of the girl; for though she had not named any name, Hellanodike felt it was Mnemarch who was pursuing her with his love. She thought of quitting the house next day and to return to her father, but there Phayllas' repulsive face encountered her and inspired her with new horror; and if she did go away, and if that could be possible which the girl hinted at, if she left him alone with Phryne,—she did not dare to follow up her thoughts, for she felt something akin to frenzy at the very idea. As she thus lay sunk back on the couch, with hands covering her face, there arose from out the garden a low, plaintive, yet inexpressibly sweet strain. It could be no one but Chlenusa, and the song she had chosen suited wonderfully with Hellanodike's sad condition; it was an old chant of Symonides, and its purport, the plaint of Danaë, driven forth by her father. A pro-

found feeling of dreamy happiness came over
Hellanodike whilst she listened to the old
strain, with closed eyes. Then the song
ceased, and she heard how Chlenusa came
gliding cautiously into the room. She kept
her eyes closed, and pretended, she hardly
knew why, to be sleeping.

Now she felt how the girl with utmost
tenderness loosened the sandals from her feet,
carefully and softly spread a cover over her;
and she then came nearer, her lips impressed
a soft kiss on her forehead, and she heard her
whispering, "Sleep, thou guileless one, the
sinner will watch over thee." With this
strange utterance Chlenusa glided out of the
room, and vanished like a shadow in the
darkling gloom of the garden.

Hardly had she closed the door behind
her which led from the women's apartments
to the forepart of the abode, when she was
met by Timoessa bearing a burning lamp.

"Well now, thou wily serpent," said she,
"hast thou slid thy poison into her heart?
Ye have tarried long together."

In the glowering eyes of the girl there gleamed a mysterious fire, but then she seemed to bethink herself of something new.

"All has been achieved even as thou didst require," she said abruptly.

"Hast thou found her sensitive? Did the creature wince?"

"Listen!" cried Chlenusa, with a hoarse voice, "if thou wouldst catch fish, I would advise thee to choose a better bait."

"What dost mean?" asked the hag spitefully.

"Well, whom else but Mnemarch? Dost thou think her simple enough to love such a man?"

"Bridle thy impudent tongue," rejoined Timoessa; "forget not that I am his mother now."

The girl burst into a scoffing laugh.

"Thou art well versed in the art of being mother to those who are not thy children; is it not so?"

"What meanest thou?" asked the old hag, threateningly advancing towards Chlenusa with uplifted hand, as if she would smite her. The girl confronted her like a panther ; her eyes started in her deathly-pale face, and her hands writhed as if they were claws. So stood the two, for a few brief seconds, speechless, then the hag slunk away, muttering.

"Had I not to think of matters more important," she said, "thou shouldst not escape unpunished for the daring insolence thou flashest at me."

With chilling scorn smiled Chlenusa, as though accustomed to such scenes, rife with threats.

"Beware, lest thou spoil our game!" said Timoessa, while doubling her bony fist. "Thou knowest our aim and how much we gain if success results as Mnemarch wishes."

"As if this were the first occasion when I have set the snare in which thou hast trapped thy game," replied Chlenusa, with the air of superiority of an ally aware that her help cannot be dispensed with.

"That is well and good. I know thou art a sly serpent," muttered the other, "but one

does not trust serpents; hast thou read in her
hands and prophesied as I ordered thee ? "

"I have told thee so ! " replied the girl,
shaking her black curls peevishly.

" She is a Bœotian," continued Timoessa,
thinking over her plan of battle, " pretty
enough certainly; and if she were an Athenian
she ought soon to be foremost of all the
hetairæ; but she has not wit enough for
that ; she is too staid, has no ambition.
Therefore the only thing left is to frighten
her; she must be made to obey from fear,
till she will not dare to wish anything else
but that which Mnemarch wishes.   Remem-
ber that," she said again, turning to Chlenusa;
" and now to bed, and go not spying about
the house."

As soon as she had gone, Chlenusa rushed
after her as far as the door, and, shaking
her fists, she spit out on the spot where
Timoessa had just been standing ; an expression of immeasurable hatred convulsing her
face.

" Thou thief ! " she hissed, with trembling

lips, "thou toad! wilt thou anew sully a
human heart with the poison of thy darksome
soul till thou canst squeeze it with thy
thievish fingers like a sponge, from out of
which the gold pieces drop into thy purse?
O curses upon thee, thou spoiler of my soul,
who calls herself my mother, which thou art
not! No," she sobbed, while sinking to the
ground; "no, do not allow it to be thus, ye
gods; avert from being true what she says,
that she, this woman, is my mother!"

She lay on the floor like one broken, and
her eyes turned involuntarily towards the
room where the beautiful girl from Tanagra,
so encompassed with danger, was reposing.
The wild face grew softer, and tears were
coursing adown her cheeks. Hitherto she
had been employed in the meanest services in
Timoessa's vile traffic, and, like a wild lynx,
had been tracking, pitilessly, all that reflected
beauty and brightness ; the hatred she
harvested therefrom she repaid by hatred,
and her soul had become filled with the
poison of envy against all above her. To-

day, at sight of the beautiful and trusting being whom she was expected to help to drag down from her pure world into the mire now surrounding her, a feeling came over her she could not understand, but which she could not put aside, because it filled her with a dim and unknown happiness. She shook her head as if wondering at herself, as if at a loss for an explanation, for as yet she knew not that love cannot be defined.

"Hallo, Polymachron!" thus exclaimed a dark curly-haired youth to one of his companions in the studio of Praxiteles, where numerous pupils of the sculptor were assembled at work, "why dost thou sit there with thy hands folded? Is the satyr there to be finished by glowering at it? There, follow the example of the Bœotian bee; look at him, the Tanagrian, how he fusses about at his Aphrodite, all diligent, without looking to right or left, without even thinking of a Kephisias,—she who never leaves thy thoughts, thou worthless favourite of Eros, whilst he has only thoughts for his glory to come, in which he will soon outshine all of us poor Athenians."

These words, intended for Myrtolaos, and which were taken up with noisy laughter by the rest of the pupils, made known the position in which he was regarded by his companions since he had been under guidance of Praxiteles.

" He is a clever being," replied Polymachron. " He wishes to be renowned, all of a sudden, and in some surprising fashion ; for that reason he now keeps his talents so far in the dark that one could almost believe they were not there at all."

Loud laughter again greeted the joke which was shot at Myrtolaos.

In silence and unheeded he let the storms of bitter mockery and sarcasm drift by. They would have harassed him but little, for well he knew they mainly sprang from the jealousy of his comrades, because of the privileged position he held with Praxiteles ; but what lent a bitter sting to those words

was that his own estimate of himself sided
with the mockery and took part against
himself.

With ardent zeal he had set to work, and
this diligence it was that had earned for him
the nickname of " the Bœotian bee ; " the first
impulse that had inspired him seemed to
promise for the best, for to his own astonishment, and to the just wonder of the master, he
developed such an inborn talent for external
treatment, that he had overcome with greatest
ease the first elements, and had tasks assigned
him greater still ; but now he had come
to a perilous pass. His fancy did not keep
pace with his technical ability; he could but
imitate the bare outlines of Praxiteles' models,
their spirit he could not grasp. Again and
again that scene flashed before his imagination when first he stood before the creations
of Praxiteles, and what had then been a
dull, indescribable feeling of trepidation, now
stood before him with more awe-inspiring
clearness—the consciousness, that his genius
had no points of contact with his master's,

that the ways of the latter were not *his* ways, and hence that the chasm separating them yawned ever wider apart. Thus a deep awe seized his soul; the feeling of an existence, that had failed in aim and purpose, began to spread its shadows through his life, and 'neath the lowering cloud that this consciousness brought into his mind, the power of invention put forth no further blossom.

Naught of this escaped the master's eyes; but he held back, for there are times when man should take counsel with himself. For Myrtolaos, however, those were moments of the most bewildering self-abasement, when he observed Praxiteles, as the latter, with saddened surprise, noticed the work of him from whom he had been expecting so much, yet received so little.

Then it befel that the youth rushed headlong into despair, cursing his hands, through whose lack of "cunning" he had been brought on the way to frenzy ; and then he cried aloud in his sore need to the gods in whom he erewhile believed

6

and he craved from them some sign as to whether he should remain leal to his calling as an artist, or should with rapid resolve cast himself loose from it. And amid these torturing conflicts uprose anew, powerful as on the first day, the irrepressible impulse towards creating and fashioning, and while he endeavoured to renounce himself, new shapes and figures were originated under his hands. But so narrow in conception, so stinted in embodiment did they appear to him when he thought in comparison of the powerful and graceful forms which grew under Praxiteles' hands, that he wrathfully shattered and trampled on his own handiworks, that he might no more have them before his eyes. All the voices that in earlier days had spoken to his soul quickened with enthusiasm, he scoffed at now with bitter scorn, for it was they that implanted in his nature qualities that rendered him unfitted for the lofty untrammelled art of Praxiteles ; they had transmuted him into an enthusiast, a dreamer secluded from

the world, had dulled his vision, so that
from out the sensual, moving world surrounding him he was unable to draw mental
nurture ; and hence did he now resolve to
break off from the memories of earlier days,
to abdicate his inmost nature, and to strive
after that which heretofore from sheer coyness he had shrunk from.

The ways and behaviour of his fellow-
students, who revelled in the unstemmed
flood of Athenian life, went against his grain ;
but from henceforth he resolved to become
one of them, to plunge into the stream, lead
whither it might; and though no Kephisias
was his, yet had he not Hellanodike ?

As this thought, coming groping as it were,
and trembling like a very criminal, from the
gloomy depths of his being, first grew upon
him, Myrtolaos was like to one who is ex-
periencing for the first time the working of
an earthquake. The feeling that the ground
whereon, as on a foundation invincible, the
structure of one's moral consciousness is built
up, may itself give way, uproots a man, and

with his living senses in all their keenness hurries him within the foreshadowings of death. Confused shapes went flitting through his brain.

Suddenly he beheld palpably before him a statue of spotless white ; it was Hellanodike. Then came two hands which clasped the fair form, and where they fastened their touch straightway appeared darksome repulsive stains, and he saw how the marble features shrank away in horror. Next it seemed to him as though two white entreating arms were stretched out to him for aid ; he shook himself free from them, and, while the limbs were sinking down, he heard clearly a wailing voice, calling on his name. Myronides' mild countenance also passed before his eyes, and gazed at him with an expression such as he had never known ; his grizzled beard was matted and begrimed.

But the thought had started into being, it loitered and took growth, and an incident befel, which was suddenly, and in a way un-looked for, to hasten it to ripeness.

Soon after the occurrence described above
there appeared in the studio of Praxiteles a
man asking for Myrtolaos from Tanagra :
it was Phayllas. At the hasty entrance of
the stranger, by the harsh tone of his voice
and the pallor of his face, the pupils of
Praxiteles perceived something unwonted was
afoot. He had not long to seek for Myrtolaos, he found him at his work.

" Myrtolaos," said he, advancing to him
without greeting, " thou knowest wherefore
I am come."

The youth looked up, a gloomy sullenness
settled on his face ; he was mute.

" Thou wouldst not hold speech with me,"
the other went on, " but thou must ; in the
name of Myronides, thou must reveal to me
where she is whom thou hast in hiding."

A general " Oh ho ! " was raised at these
words among the art-students ; they put their
heads together, laughed, and made merry at
having surprised the secret of this Bœotian
busy-bee.

" I know that she has fled away after

thee," cried Phayllas, now quickened to
wrath by the other's silence; "and I tell thee,
I go not forth without her. Despoiler and
betrayer, where hast thou Hellanodike?
Restore her to me!"

He had grasped Myrtolaos by the
shoulder and shook him. With a sudden
movement the latter drew himself up, flung
aside from his shoulder the grasp of his
opponent, and, while fastening his flaming
eyes on the death-pale face, exclaimed,—

"Never shalt thou have back Hellanodike,
never!"

In his lithe beauty he stood there, in prime
of youth and vigour, like to a wrathful Apollo.

Fickle as people often are, and especially
as was the case with Athenians of that day,
the feeling of his fellows in art veered
suddenly round in favour of the handsome
Tanagrian.

"Look at him!" called out tawny Lysias.
"By the gods, look at the Tanagrian,—what
a glorious build he has! Only stay standing
so, glory of my eyes, and I fashion after thee

a Dioskuros that shall make thee and me immortal."

"Bravo, Myrtolaos!" exclaimed Polyma-chron. "Let not thy maiden be snatched from thee, we stick by thee for Hellanodike!"

A wild boisterous uproar came resounding as answering cry from the others.

"Ye Athenian youths!" returned Phayllas, pallid and trembling from excitement, to the pupil, 'not so would ye speak did ye but know how he hath demeaned himself; when I tell you that from his foster-father, at whose board for long years he ate and in whose home he dwelt, he hath stolen away his only darling child."

"Who tells thee I have done this? who confers on thee the right to slander me?" cried Myrtolaos, with thundering voice. "Stolen her have I not; of her own free choice she followed me, to fly from thee whom she hates."

"She shows taste, and I must give her praise," interrupted Lysias, "if she prefers him to thee, thou jealous lover!"

"Think you I will submit to it," said
Phayllas, who, instead of one, suddenly saw
so many enemies confronting him, "that he
shall lower to be his mere plaything the
maiden whom I thought to make my wife?"

"Who dares say this to thee?" cried
Myrtolaos, doubling his fist in his face.

"I am fully aware of it," rejoined
Phayllas ; "for I know thee, and have the
conviction that thou art a betrayer and despoiler of hearts." The long pent-up hatred
broke forth, cutting like a dagger that
has at last reached its yearned-for aim.

"Hear me!" turning yet again to the
scholars of Praxiteles. "You are listening
to the voice of justice, lead me to Praxiteles ; he is a right-thinking man, he will
tell me where I shall find the misguided
maiden."

"Praxiteles?" shouted scoffingly tawny
Lysias. "Thinkest thou he has time
to fluster himself about our sweethearts?
Scud off home, I advise thee, Bœotian, and
forget not this is Athens, and that thou

art a stranger in Athens. Praxiteles is in
the country."

" If from the stranger you would withhold
his right, reflect withal," said Phayllas,
"that this youth also and the maiden too
are equally strangers in Athens; it is a
mere contest between strangers."

" Bad shot, Bœotian ! " taunted Polymachron ; "he is a scholar of Praxiteles, and
whoso can venture to entitle himself thus,
has become an Athenian."

"He is an Athenian ! " shouted they in
chorus ; " Myrtolaos is an Athenian ! "

" And the scholars of Praxiteles stand up
for one another, bear in mind ! " said one
sturdy-limbed companion, who from among the
group advanced threatening towards Phayllas.

" Aye, everything else they may take,
only not our sweethearts."

" Nay, by the gods, whoso dare even to lay
finger on Kephisias," laughed Polymachron.

" And once for all," pronounced Lysias,
" Hellanodike is his, and so does she remain."

A noisy taunting cry stormed down the words of Phayllas. Tears of impotent rage flowed down his cheeks, for he saw no prospect of attaining to his end.

He shook his fist towards Myrtolaos.

"Well then," he exclaimed, "if it be true that yon wench is sunk so low that she of her own accord followed in thy traces, get thee gone to her and bear her the curse of her grey-haired father, whom she hath turned into the laughing-stock of his town, and whom she hath cast into sorrow and despair,—and all for thy sake, thou utter villain!"

"List not to that croaking raven," broke out tawny Lysias,—"and out from here with thee, thou jealous bleating he-goat!"

"Out with him! out with him!" The whole wild crew went straight for Phayllas. "Out and away with him back to Bœotia, where he may go nibble thistles, the braying donkey!"

Sturdy fists grasped him on all sides; a

minute later Phayllas found himself outside
the studio spun round like a top on
himself, and strided forward along the dust
of the street. In the doorway stood
Lysias, hurling threats after him.

"If we find thee sneaking any longer
hereabouts, or if thou dost make any
endeavour behind our back to reach
Praxiteles, then hadst thou best look about
for another skull, since the one thou
bearest on thy shoulders thou bringst not
safe and sound to thy home again."

Phayllas rose up, beat the dust from his
garments, and, without turning, slunk
speechless away, like to a loathsome spider
bloated with venom.

Myrtolaos at one stroke had become the
hero of the day. He whom they had
taken for a sullen sulker had an adventure
to flaunt in the light of day such as no
one among his companions could boast,—
that worked an impression ; and while the
others were not able to vaunt loud enough
about their sweethearts, he had kept en-

shrined his treasure in coy reserve—that above all bore off the palm.

And as he to his companions seemed now quite another being, so had his demeanour changed towards them, since he had seen them so powerfully upholding his wishes. He was an equal amongst equals, and the vigorous feeling which the consciousness of belonging to those who are like-minded awakened came for the first time with full power over him. An undefined impulse seized him, and to relieve his full heart he sprang on his work-stool, and :—"Evoë for Hellanodike!" he cried with joyous shout into the hall.

"Evoë for Myrtolaos and Hellanodike!" came echoed the laughing reply.

"No more work to-day," said Polymachron, flinging his chisel into the corner. "At the inn outside the gates at Ilissos some excellent young wine has arrived from Thasos, and a covey of field-fares was trapped this morning in the nets of our excellent host, Phaedimos ; come, let us away thither, and celebrate our victory by a joyous banquet."

The idea found rapturous approval ; the work-a-day trim was doffed, and soon after the whole troop hied to the town-gates towards the inn lying outside.

On the way Polymachron halted.

" Brothers," said he, " are we like Scythians or Paphlagonians, to dine without the added delight of our charming sweet-hearts. I will call for Kephisias ; each of ye do likewise, and let Myrtolaos make us acquainted with Hellanodike."

This proposal was the more welcome, since after what had occurred that morning all were naturally eager to look upon Hellano-dike's fair form. Myrtolaos seemed to ponder for a while, but there was no means of evading the urging of his comrades, who had now, in some measure, earned a claim to look upon his beloved, and besides there had come a feeling of inward delight that allowed no scope for reflection.

" Go you forward," he cried, " we shall find

you;" and he proceeded towards Mnemarchos' house, which was situated not far from the foot of the Acropolis.

It was lucky for him Mnemarch, who had of late shown him no very friendly mien as often as he had visited Hellanodike, was not at his home. Hellanodike had just refreshed herself with the bath, and never had she appeared to him more fascinating and graceful than now, as she joyously starting up on his entering the garden, ran forward to embrace him.

He pressed her to his heart, and kissed off the last glittering diamond drops that beaded like dew her brown locks, and as he thought this charming being, severed from father and home, was now exclusively and solely his own, he felt his heart expand with rapture indescribable.

" Hellanodike," he said, "my sweet darling, my beloved, now at last I have won thee wholly for myself. Knowest thou who was with me to-day ? "

She glanced at him inquiringly.

" Phayllas, who required that I should
surrender thee to him."

" Phayllas ? " she exclaimed, all trembling ;
" what answer didst thou give him ? "

" Canst thou ask ?—that he never should
possess thee, never ! Or should I mayhap
have said otherwise ? " he went on, as he
saw her eyes brimming over with silent
tears.

" Nay," she replied, gently nestling closer
to him, " nay ; but thou knowest, my father,
——" and her tears flowed more copiously.

" Weep not," he said tenderly ; " it was
to happen even as it has come to pass. Thou
art aware I would not rob thy father of
thee, but free we are from the odious
Phayllas ; therefore, let us rejoice."

" And he knows not where I am ? " she
asked, timidly.

"He does not know, and never shall," he
said assuringly. " And now look yonder," and
he pointed over the walls of the garden
towards the Acropolis, where the golden-
pointed spear of Athene Promachos was

glittering in the glorious heaven, " look how she points upward to the warm glowing heavens, as if to say, behold them and enjoy ; the world lies before us, offering a wide scene for our love. Come, we will soar across like unto two happy cooing doves. I will show it thee, and thou shalt be quickened with joy when thou shalt become conscious how sweet life tastes, if one but spend it in Athens."

Gladness of heart made him eloquent, and its rapture was reflected from his face to Hellanodike's.

" O thou faithless, dearly-loved Myrtolaos," she exclaimed, with fascinating smile, " so thou hast already forgotten about Athens ? Who knows thou wilt bring matters so far with thy sweet words as to drive all thoughts of my native town from my heart ? "

With arms entwined they were wandering round the court. Suddenly Chlenusa appeared. She glanced keenly at Myrtolaos, and then said curtly,—

glimmering in the glorious heaven, & hand how she points upward to the warm glowing heavens, as if to say, behold them and enjoy ; the world lies before us, offering a wide space for our love.   Come, we will soar across like unto two happy cooing doves.   I will show it thee, and thou shalt be quickened with joy when thou shalt become conscious how sweet life tastes, if one but spend it in Athens."

[illegible line]
[illegible line]
Halbarnimbes.

"O thou faithless, dearly-beloved Meromlea," she exclaimed, with [illegible] smile, as thou hast already forgotten about Athens ; Who knows thou will bring matters so far with thy sweet words as to drive all thoughts of my native town from my heart ?"

With arms entwined they were wandering round the court. Suddenly [illegible] appeared. She glanced keenly at Myrmelea, and then said aloud,—

" Timoessa is coming."

At the same instant the old hag entered, and approached the two with cringing civility.

" Visitor come, as I see ?   The handsome pupil of Praxiteles here again.   That is right ; our dove lives a lonely life, for my son is anxious to have a reputable house. Now, how goes it with the divine master Praxiteles, and Phryne his adorable friend ? "

With gratification she noticed that Myrtolaos blushed, and that a shade passed over Hellanodike's countenance.

" Good mother," Myrtolaos interrupted, " I come to rob thee of thy ward, and to show her something of Athens."

" That is right," said Timoessa, growing attentive.   " What have ye in hand ?   Whither are ye bent ? "

" We have prepared a little feast outside the walls, at Phædimos'.   Thou wilt not object to it, nor will thy son Mnemarchos either, as I hope, if I invite Hellanodike to the feast ? "

7

A momentary hideous grin played round the puckered folds of the toothless mouth.

"To Phædimos at Ilissos? Ah, I know naught of him, yet have I heard sometimes of his repute. Ye will have a fine time of it, ye sons of Praxiteles, eh? Well, of course Hellanodike is free, free as a bird that can fly whither it will. Go with him, my dove, be joyous and of good heart. Life is short, and one must take advantage of its happy moments. I will let my son know of the plans, and he will surely be glad to hear that our little dove is delighting herself in good company."

She seemed quite enchanted, and only the impatient mien of the youth checked her from letting her tongue run wild once more.

"Ye are speedful," she said, with submissive demeanour, "and I will not detain you."

With these words she vanished, and left the lovers all bewildered.

"Thou wilt lead me to Ilissos?" cried

Hellanodike, happy as a child. "Come, I will get ready."

She disappeared into her chamber, and a moment after returned in a long robe that flowed down to her feet, and with a round low-crowned hat on her head.

"I must take shame to myself before the Athenians," she said, "should I appear before them in my Tanagrian head-gear."

Instead of further answer, he twined his arm about her, led her to the brink of the brook, and showed her, in the dark mirror, her image.

"Thinkest thou that she who looketh so need take shame before any mortal in the world?"

She gazed content at the "counterfeit presentment" in all its sweet attraction. Thereafter appeared his countenance likewise in the water. She signed to him; he nodded back. They fell into each other's arms, and were as two happy laughing children

Chlenusa had meanwhile, without apparently giving heed to what was uttered and

done, been busying herself with her distaff.
As Myrtolaos with Hellanodike were now
leaving the garden, casting her distaff aside
she came suddenly towards them.

" Something I have to beg of thee," she
said to Hellanodike, who looked at her
bewildered.

" I pray thee," and she stammered somewhat, " go not to Phædimos on the Ilissos."

" Wherefore should she not?" cried Myrtolaos.

" Why?" and she glanced keenly and
steadfastly at him, " because bad folk come
there yonder."

" What sort dost mean?" continued the
youth.

" It were better thou askedst not ; but
believe me they are folks to whose circle she
doth not belong ; believe me that I know it,
for many a time, and oftener than thou, have
I been in the tavern on the Ilissos."

" Verily, then," he said angrily, " the company must have been bad enough;" and he
glanced spurningly at the girl.

A deep flush crimsoned her face.

"Thou dost wrong to wound me," she said, turning her flashing eyes towards him, "since I advise for thy best, for her best"—and she motioned with her head towards Hellanodike—"is also thy best ; is it not so?" She spoke the last slowly, and with strangely-measured tone. Despite himself he reddened.

"Hast thou not heard what Timoessa said? Will she likely know Phædimos less than thou ?"

The girl broke into a hoarse laugh.

"Timoessa," she cried, "Timoessa, ah !" She shook impatiently her head, and looked at him as one regards him touching whom one knows not whether he cannot understand, or will not understand.

"Come forth," exclaimed Myrtolaos, with impatience, "I know not what the girl wants."

He would fain with Hellanodike have passed by her, but Chlenusa barred the way to the door.

"Hear me !" and her voice rang shrill, as

from inner emotion, while, as though she
would hold fast Hellanodike, she caught hold
of the arms of the latter with both hands.
"Go not to the Ilissos, for if thou goest——"
She became dumb-stricken; it was as though
the words had throttled her.

"Well, what then, if she does go?" cried
Myrtolaos, while Hellanodike looked in
speechless wonder at the passionate girl;
"what then, in short, if she goes? Speak
out clearly!"

With a spring Chlenusa was at the door
of issue, bent her head down listening, then
laid a finger on her mouth, snatching at the
hem of Hellanodike's robe, drew her and
Myrtolaos hurriedly to the farthest part of
the courtyard. Her breast heaved as if
tortured with cramp, and her eyes were
peering around in anxiety.

"Lost is she," she whispered hoarsely,
"abandoned without help or saving,—and I
will not have it, I will not!" and she fell down
at Hellanodike's feet, and hid her face in the
folds of her robe, now bathed in tears.

" Wherefore lost ? abandoned to whom ? " asked Myrtolaos, roughly.

" Abandoned to the master of this house," she returned, with her eyes fixed on the door of issue, as though she feared every moment lest some one might enter and surprise her while busied upon the dreadful secret.

" Mnemarchos !" cried Hellanodike out of herself.

" Oh, by the gods, speak soft," she entreated ; " yea, Mnemarch. Listen, thou must learn it now ; that witch, Timoessa, is not his mother. Like a wolf he slinks around thee here ; his impure thoughts have a thousand times already got upon the track which he himself has not yet happened on, because he is filled with awe in presence of a woman clothed in chastity, and in dread of the verdict of the people, which would inflict punishment on him for any deed of violence towards a woman unspotted."

" What way dost thou mean ? " asked Hellanodike, trembling.

Chlenusa started up and whispered one word in her ear; a deathly pallor spread over the countenance of Hellanodike; she shuddered and——

"What has she said to thee?" cried Myrtolaos, holding her in his arms.

"Oh ! silence," she whispered, "silence, it is too awful to say it!"

"Not yet has he dared," Chlenusa continued, passionately and impressively; "but if thou goest without the walls to Phædimos, he will have the audacity to risk it. Know, then, the inn at Ilissos is ill-famed through all Athens; only hetairæ there do congregate."

"Hetairæ?" and Hellanodike drew back, shuddering.

"Yea, yea, hetairæ; and if it comes to his ears that thou hast been in their midst, then he need no longer be afraid of any one; then he will treat thee as one, and then— then——"

"Enough, enough ; be silent !" Myrtolaos interrupted. He paced up and down the

court ; a black tempest was raging in his
heart ; then he approached Chlenusa.

" Dost know what I will now do ?" said
he, with folded arms ; " all thou hast
spoken I will repeat to Mnemarch."

She stared at him wildly, with a strange,
chilling smile playing on her lips.

" Thou wilt repeat all to Mnemarchos ?"

" That I will ; and what dost think will
be the consequence?"

" I will tell thee," she said, hoarsely ;
" then they will scourge me."

" Very possibly," he replied.

" And maybe," she continued, " they will
keep it up so long till they kill me."

" And thou wilt certainly have deserved it
well," was his wrathful answer.

A hoarse, broken cry was rent from her
bosom, she shook her black streaming locks
from her bronze face.

" Fool," she cried, " for still I believe that
thou art only foolish, not wicked ; and then
there will be no one left to guard her who
loves thee, and whom thou wouldst imperil,

like a vile coward ! No one, no one !" She
clasped her hands before her face, and broke
out in heart-rending weeping.

An awful silent pause ensued.

Then Hellanodike slowly took off her hat,
and approached Chlenusa.

" Weep not," she said, and her snowy hand
was laid on the dark dishevelled hair, " I will
not go to Phædimos, and he will not say
word to Mnemarchos; do thou now depart."

" Thou wilt not ?" said Myrtolaos, after
Chlenusa had gone. She drooped her head.

" I think it would be better were I not to
go."

His face grew sombre, he bit his lips in
silence.

" Myrtolaos," said she, placing her hands
on his shoulders, and looking into his eyes,
" couldst thou really wish it still ? "

" Why dost thou open heart and ears to
the fancies of this mad girl?" he said,
abruptly.

" But if it were possible that she spoke

truth? if really such women——" Her modest face was suffused with blushes, and she could not pronounce the word.

" They are not hetairæ," he said, " they are friends of the artists ; folks who know nothing about it may think wrongly of them, but I have told thee what their position really is."

She bowed down her face, and her breast heaved in silent agony.   He came close to her, and grasped both her hands.

" Hellanodike," said he, " he who wants to learn the art of Praxiteles must venture upon the stormy sea of life, and must not be afraid if the shore disappear from his vision for a brief space !   Look at the works of this man ; they have all but one law and one measure,— that which nature dictates !   But they scorn the narrow mind that is afraid of them, for they are like nature, which is mirrored in itself, and does not ask whether we look at it with eyes unsullied or impure. Hellanodike," he said, and his dark eyes flashed with a devouring fire, " I cannot

expect to rise into the Olympian sphere of this
art, if I cannot, like other artists, quaff from
the fountain of life I long for.   I thirst after
it, for I see it before me; I breathe its air,
but when I want to stoop down it evades my
burning lips."

He had put his arm round her, and felt
how her slender form trembled while he
pressed her to his heart.

"Oh!" she murmured, "that I could
understand thee!"

He let go her arm and stepped back a
little.

"Thou dost not understand me?" he said;
"thou dost not feel that I can no longer live
thus, always separated from thee, only for
brief moments with thee; that thou ought to
be with me always, ever, because I have need
of thee, like to the air I breathe and from
which I cannot sever myself, if I would live?"

She lifted her great beseeching eyes
heavenward, and wrung her hands.

"Oh that I had been born in Athens,
and had grown up in this air," said she, "or

that thou hadst never seen me, or known me, in Tanagra, it would have been better alike for thee and me!"

"No," he replied; "for it only depends on thy will, if on it is to depend our happiness."

"Have mercy on me," cried she; "I would do all thou wishest, but this I can not do, Myrtolaos, I cannot!"

Her bosom rose and fell fitfully; and one saw that she was standing on a borderland which even love does not allow to be traversed, for her inborn nature built up a firm stronghold of defence.

He turned silently away, and was about to go.

"Myrtolaos!" she cried, in agonised tones.

He stood still, she rushed up to him and fell on his neck.

"Thou goest," she sobbed, "and when wilt thou return?"

He looked at her confusedly.

"I see thy heart," said she despairingly, "how it turns away from her that cannot understand thee. I know thou wilt cease

loving me, in order to find among Athenian
women what she was unable to afford; and
then what remains to her who followed
thee from Tanagra, because she put trust
in thee whom she loved?"

Overcome by her sorrow she lay in his
arms, weak as a flower that a thundershower
has bowed to earth. He gazed down upon
her, and beheld a fulness of beauty that rested
in his arms, such as no Phryne could offer.
But tears he saw;—the divine creations
of Praxiteles wept not, and sorrow and
anguish were not the models by which they
had been inspired.

"Weep not," he said, and yet he had
a feeling as if he had no right to check
those tears; "may the gods show us a way
out of these perplexities and anxieties!"

He loosed her arms from his neck, and
went his way.

At the water's edge, on the very spot
where the reflection of her form had greeted
his own, Hellanodike sat down, and the

unsympathetic element drank in her tears just as quietly as it had reflected her smiles. With a gloomy heart, and senses all aglow, Myrtolaos wended his way to the tavern on the Ilissos.

A sombre feeling of rancour against Hellanodike glided into his heart, and he began to feel as if she were a burden to him that held his imagination in bonds. He bethought him of her tears, but they touched his heart no longer ; they only seemed to him but as an expression of the alarm which hearts of ice experience before love dawns ; he felt himself sundered from her who would fain remain a Bœotian, and not become an Athenian ; and he thought of her words, that he would find consolation amongst Athenian women. He stamped his foot.

" Thy prophecy," he murmured, " may get fulfilled ! "

At Phædimos the feast was already in full swing, and he found himself straightway

drawn into the wild whirlpool. The first
question was, of course, why he had not
brought Hellanodike.

"She is ill," he answered curtly.

"Ill," exclaimed a voluptuous being who
planted herself next him, and without further
ado threw her arms round his neck. "I
will comfort thee, thou lonely boy;" and
upon his lips, yet fresh from the pressure
of the sweet mouth that had a moment
agone touched his, now burned the glowing
kiss of the hetaira. The beauty of the
youth charmed the eyes and senses of the
women, so that he was soon encompassed
by them, and had to use force to free himself from their endearments.

A goblet of Thasistan wine was set before
him; he drained it off; a second and a third
followed, and the dark harassing doubts
that had kept haunting him were merged in
the sparkling flow.

Suddenly, as from a dream, he started
up, and thumping on the table with his
fist, he cried,—

"By the gods, this is Athens!"

A loud laugh burst from all present. "Hast thou doubted it, beautiful Tanagrian?" said the black-eyed Kephisias, leaning against his shoulder, and gazing at him with laughing eyes.

"Before I beheld thee, yes," he replied, "but from henceforth, seest thou, I doubt no longer."

He put his arms round her neck, imprinting kisses on her cheeks and eyes, till Polymachron from the other end of the table called out, "Hullo!"

"Never mind!" cried Lysias soothingly, "thou canst make it good with Hellanodike."

A burst of laughter arose, and Myrtolaos laughed outright.

The feeding and drinking went on within doors, and gradually a sultry heat pervaded the place. Myrtolaos, less accustomed than his companions to carousing, went forth to court the cooling breezes on the borders of the Ilissos.

8

returned home. Up to the brink of the sea
by the Phaleron his unrest had driven him ;
his limbs were mortally broken with fatigue,
and he had found no repose. All that
had harassed him returned with redoubled
vigour ; he had tried to shake off his own
nature, and that moment had taught him it
was a useless sacrilege, as shake it off he
could not. But his nature, as he now from
experience knew, could never lead him there
where Praxiteles had taken his stand.

He saw no way out from this dilemma,
and despair came upon him. On the threshold of the house he met Praxiteles, and
both stood. still, struck with each other's
appearance.

Like to a demoniacal being endowed with
powers supernatural, so did the master seem
to the youth. What he could not achieve
by the sacrifice of his own individual nature,
this man possessed utterly, and the fiery look
of his clear glance revealed that he had not
had to surrender anything, that he needed
not to court the impure, in order to be able

to achieve. Had he, then, battled through the strife even as his pupil was now doing? Or were there natures so entirely different from his own as that the fervour of passion was with them transmuted into the fervour of feeling?

Not less wonder-struck did Praxiteles look at Myrtolaos, in whose features the mental excitement of the last hours had left deep traces. The beautiful boy-face had matured through earnest conflict, and from the eyes, erewhile so happy and so dreamy, a silent and reproachful consciousness peered forth, and on his forehead discouragement had graven deep broad furrows.

" Like Hermes," said to himself Praxiteles, "like Hermes returning from Hades, and revolving its horrors in his mind;" and he advanced to Myrtolaos and took him by the hand. " Come," said he, " this hour is the right one; to-day the Olympic Hermes must be created."

The youth followed him in silence ; against this man he had no inner power of re-

sistance.   But a   feeling of desolateness
crept into his heart.   He would have cast
himself at Praxiteles' feet, and besought him
in his distressful mood ; but he was become
to him nought save a study for his artistic
fancies, and every line that anguish graved
on his face rendered this study all the more
precious.

Arrived at the master's studio, which lay
some distance from that of the pupils, Praxiteles told him to put off his garment, and
he then assigned him the position in which
he thought of representing him.   The mind·
of the artist seemed to have been working
beforehand, for in a brief space the finest
position was hit upon which the noble
frame might assume.   The left arm reposed
on a truncated column, while the right, uplifted, was to clasp the Hermes' staff ; the
head was bent downward somewhat dreamily.
And now the work was entered on.

Myrtolaos had not yet seen Praxiteles
busied in his art ; he now looked on at him
in wonderment ; with a restlessness and

withal a sureness, as if every limb were
controlled by springs of steel, he grasped
the clay wherewith he began to model; and
when he turned his eyes on the youth to
read off the lines from his frame, Myrtolaos
seemed to feel the burning influence of those
eyes; they were like diamonds cutting
through glass.

Hour sped on after hour, and ceaseless
still was Praxiteles toiling on.

No word was uttered, and the only sound
noticeable was the slight panting of the youth,
on whom the tension of the sleepless night
had brought sheer exhaustion.

Praxiteles paused not, nor observed the
face growing paler and paler. Dumb-struck,
and with a feeling akin to awe, Myrtolaos
gazed upon the man who was as intent upon
his work as a tiger over his prey.

So pitiless, equally towards himself and
others, must the man be constituted who would
fashion his creatures like Praxiteles; a dawning perception came to him of the holy awe
surrounding Art, which is so gentle in its

aims, yet so cruel in the pursuit thereof; he
grew conscious that his soft heart would never
possess that hardness of adamant ; a dusky,
giddying phantasm floated like a grey cloud
from the depths of his heart upward to his
eyes ; it seemed to him as if he were like
metal wherefrom a statue is to be cast, merged
in the glow of a molten mass—he felt the
very torture of annihilation.

" I can no more ! " he broke forth suddenly,
with sinking voice ; his head drooped down,
and in the swooning that befel, he would
have fallen heavily to earth had not Praxi-·
teles caught him.

While placing him on a couch, the sculptor
glanced for the first time at the sun ; it was
already long past midday.

When Myrtolaos recovered from his swoon
and opened his still half-veiled eyes, he beheld
a womanly form bending over him, and a soft
hand supporting his wearied head.

" Hellanodike ? " he whispered, gently.

" Not Hellanodike," came the laughing
reply ; he looked and recognised Phryne.

" Poor Hermes ! " she said. " I know
what it is to fall into the hands of that awful
being; he kills us in order to make us immortal.''

She raised a cup to his lips and poured in
some drops of wine, so that he found anew
his exhausted powers.

" Is he again among us ? " asked Praxiteles,
who got up from his work. He came near
and laid his hand on the pale forehead of the
youth.

" Poor boy," he said, with a smile, " the
strain was too much for thee, thou hadst not
yet taken any food."

" And on what dost thou live ? " cried
Phryne, as she raised her eyes to Praxiteles ;
" for I know that thou in like manner hast
taken not an atom the livelong day."

" I ? " exclaimed Praxiteles ; he laughed
outright, right merrily, and fell to his work
anew.

" By the gods," said she, " he is no man;
he is rather one from the lower world of
spirits."

She came behind him, and as he took no notice she laid her hands on his shoulders, and glanced over them at the wonderful creations that were growing under his hand.

" Thou magician ! " she whispered, with deep wonderment, and leaned her cheek against his. He looked up now, threw his brown, sinewy arm round her, and drew her to his knee. While he looked into her face, and divined the rapture in her thrilling features, which gathered from the outward seeming of the dawning work, of art its very essence, he sprang up with a cry of delight, that, un-restrained, burst from him ; he caught the fair form in his powerful arms, and slightly pushing her forward, as lightly as a child, let her sink back on his throbbing breast, while she imprinted on his face the kisses of a Bac-chante. From his couch the pallid Myrtolaos looked on, all bewildered, at this sight ; like to bounding lion cubs, rejoicing in their free-dom, so seemed they to him,—a freedom that to all not of lion nature appeared savagery unrestrained.

At length, Phryne, with heightened colour and panting breath, came back to him.

"Hermes," she said, "yet one word more, and a comfort for thee ; to-morrow we keep high festival. The ambassadors from Cnidos are coming to take away the Aphrodite that Praxiteles has executed for them; we shall entertain them as guests, and invite Mnemarch and yet another—knowest thou whom ? "

He sank his eyes in silence.

" Down-hearted Tanagrian ! " said she, as she took his curly head between her hands, " to-morrow thou shalt become joyous again."

It was on the morning of the next day that people were thronging before Mnemarchos' house.

" What is afloat ? " asked passers-by.

" She has gone into the house," was the answer.

"She ? Who ? "

" Well who else ? Phryne."

That was enough; and like flies clinging to

the honeyed stick, the Athenians, ever longing
for the sight of beauty, loitered at the door to
wait for the moment when she should again
come out ; for the day when one had seen
Phryne, the favourite of the town, was not a
lost one, even though one had to wait about
on the pavement from sunrise to sunset.

Hellanodike stood in the garden-court and
listened to the muffled, swelling noise without, and now she started up; for into the
garden there stepped a woman, such as she
had never before beheld. From the dainty
foot to the laughing eyes, all was beaming
life, sweetness, and beauty; and had she not
guessed who the stranger was, she would
have learned it from Mnemarch's lips, for
he heralded the visitor, and loaded her with
inane flatteries.

"Divine Phryne," he cried, "thou dost
honour to my house. They will say that the
sun with the morning star have met in my
humble abode ; " and he looked with blinking
eyes towards Hellanodike, who had remained
coyly in the background of the court.

Without further heeding him, Phryne went straight towards Hellanodike.

"Hellanodike," she said, "the daughter of Myronides of Tanagra?" and she held out her hand in greeting.

Silently the other placed her own in it.

"I perceive," she replied, "that thou knowest me." She uplifted her eyes, and the two women looked for a moment in silence at one another. It was a look full of significance. Beautiful women cannot stand side by side with indifference; they must become either friends or foes; and the instinct of the heart, that inborn power of nature, is more strongly developed in women than in man, because they are less freed from unconscious nature, which imparts to their minds a quicker apprehension of the feelings of a kindred nature than is given to the mind of man.

Majestic, and towering half a head above the other, and in more developed fulness of beauty, stood Phryne beside the tender maidenly figure, and yet, as she glanced down to the humbly drooping head, she felt that

in the most hidden recess of that timid soul
there was a something which seemed to say
to her, the triumphant Phryne: " Stand
aside from me; " that power born of meek-
ness, which can subdue a world,—gracious
maidenhood. To be made conscious
thereof, and to resolve almost unwittingly
to bear down this resistance, was but as a
flash of time in the heart of the woman
so wont to conquer.

" I am come to invite thee," she said ;
" Praxiteles gives a banquet to the ambassadors of Cnidos and to Myrtolaos, thy friend
and ours ; the banquet would afford no
pleasure wert thou not present."

A blush crimsoned Hellanodike's face
and neck.

In the tone of these words, seeming to
treat her love for Myrtolaos as a thing of
every-day import, as a simple matter of
course, there was something that repelled
and revolted her. The chaste secret of
her heart was a secret now no longer ;
strange eyes had pried into it, and had

drawn their own conclusions as to what seemed to them right.

" Women at table with men ? " she asked, with forced smile. In her father's house that would have seemed impossible in her eyes.

" Ah, I know," Phryne replied, " that to Greek women it seems a violation of laws eternal to leave the women's apartments and go among men. What folly ! Have we not sprung from the hands of one and the same nature, and does difference of sex involve enmity between them ? Never ; for completion is the law that rules man and woman. Yea, I love men, for I gladly bask in the rays which shine from the eyes of the man of genius ; I like to tremble before such mighty power; and I laugh at women who upbraid me for that I think thus and act as I think ; and I love women, too, for in their beauty I reverence the great law of harmony made visible, which checks the unbridled man, and prompts the idle to action. And just as I despise the man who

withdraws himself from this mighty influence, so am I angered with the Grecian
women who, in foolish timidity, hide themselves from men, instead of learning to
understand the decree the gods have written
in flaming letters on their glowing frames,
instead of coming amongst men and trans-
muting such as are uncouth into courteous
beings, and making of this world an Elysium,
in which passions only waken to glow, but
no longer consume the powers vying with each
other,—wrestle with merely, but no longer
destroy each other in deadly feud. Come,
I pray !" Her voice grew melodious and
caressing, and she twined her arm about the
still flushed neck of the girl. " Why dost
thou fear ? Fear is such an ugly worm
in the sweet-smelling rose of life's gladness.
Come, go with me, try the charm caused
by the eyes of noble men lighting up at thy
beauty, and when thou standest in their
midst like unto a star, whose presence is
merit enough in itself ; or dost thou believe,"
and her tone grew more earnest, " that any

but noble men frequent the house of Praxiteles ? or perhaps he has not yet told thee that thou mayest well dare to appear before the eyes of all judges of beauty, and say, ' Pronounce your verdict ! ' "

Placing her hand under Hellanodike's chin, she lifted up the maiden's head, looking roguishly into her eyes.

Despite herself Hellanodike smiled in return, as the flashing dark eyes glanced into her own; and Phryne had triumphed.

She clapped her hands with delight.

" Mnemarchos," she said, turning to him, who had followed everything with the closest attention, " gather up all the wit and spirit thou art master of, that this day thou mayest be worthy to dine in company with the two most beautiful women of Athens."

Mnemarch bowed with honeyed smile.

" And now no dallying," continued Phryne, addressing Hellanodike ; " I will take thee from here to our abode, and will myself play the part of tire-woman, to adorn thee fittingly."

9

" Thou wouldst of thyself?" said Hellanodike.

" Oh, thou shalt see how far I have learned
from the sculptors."

While Mnemarch withdrew, the two
women went to Hellanodike's chamber and
chose the garments and ornaments Phryne
thought suiting the day's festival. She took
the matter in real earnest, and it lasted some
time till she had carried out the work to
her heart's content.

At last the adorning was completed, and
no artist could to better advantage have set
off the lovely youthful figure than Phryne's
hands had done.

"But one ornament is now wanting," she
said, as she stood before her arranging the
last folds of the light blue upper garment
flowing around Hellanodike's slender form ;
" how comes it, did he not bring thee the
armlet I gave him for thee ? "

" It was too wide for my arm," replied
Hellanodike, blushing ; " there it is."

A saucy look flashed from Phryne's eyes.

" Oh, really too wide ? " she said ; "was it not perceived that it can be made smaller ? "

The armlet, wrought of finest gold, could be pressed together, in fact, so that the links, instead of joining, overlapped. In this manner Phryne fastened the gem round Hellanodike's left arm ; the cold metal touched her skin, and a tremor passed through her.

Phryne held up the beautiful limb for a moment.

" Thou lovely one ! " said she, then, letting the arm drop, she imprinted a sudden kiss on the round white shoulder, which, soft and full, peeped out from under the garment.

The gates were thrown open, and Phryne and Hellanodike stepped out into the street, the former placing her arm on Hellanodike's shoulder.

The latter shrank back on hearing the loud shouts of joy that greeted them at this moment.

" Courage ! " whispered Phryne, smilingly ;

"these good Athenians are a little boisterous when they are pleased."

With majestic bearing she stepped through the crowd surrounding them.

A sunburnt fellow, half boy, half youth, made himself specially prominent by his zeal. He walked before the women like a herald, glancing round from time to time with gleaming eyes, and smilingly showing his white teeth.

"All hail to the godlike hetairæ, all hail to the beautiful Phryne!" he screamed with fanatic exultation, and the cry was repeated by the crowd, "All hail to the godlike hetairæ!"

Hellanodike trembled all over.

"The insolent ones," she whispered, "hearst thou what they are saying?"

Phryne laughed, and drew her arm closer round Hellanodike's shoulder.

"Who can the other be who is with her?" said a middle-aged man to his companion, so loud that Hellanodike could hear each word. "She is hardly less beautiful than Phryne."

"I know not," replied the other. "Most

likely a new hetaira, intended to add to the array in Praxiteles' Olympus."

"Happy Olympian," said the first speaker, and both laughed.

Hellanodike's face was suffused with blushes, the ground on which she walked seemed to her like molten metal, and she hardly dared to lift her eyes.

Like a release to her it seemed, when at last they reached the house of Praxiteles.

The fetching-away of the great work of art by the delegates from Cnidos was an event, for it proved anew the intellectual supremacy of Athens over the rest of Greece. In the earlier hours of noon a solemn ceremony had taken place before the assembled council of the town, to welcome the delegates; the feast at the artist's house, and the actual handing over of the masterpiece was to wind up the matter, and the first citizens of the town had been bidden as guests to the feast.

Slaves now came running from the Acropolis with the news that the solemn proces-

sion was on the way ; in Praxiteles' house
might be heard the loud-sounding clangour
from the bronze disc, hung up in the peristyle;
the slaves, adorned for the feast, gathered
round the entrance of the house ; then came,
accompanied by the three Archons, by the
chief men of the town, and by other well-to-
do citizens, the Cnidian ambassadors. At the
threshold of the house the host advanced towards them, and greeted them with dignified
courtesy.

A perfume of fresh flowers was wafted
through the whole house ; in the vestibule, in
which they entered first, all the most perfect
works of the sculptor were arrayed ; and
wherever one looked, the eye rested on
arrangements in such exquisite taste, that
the guests felt as if they had been transported
into a loftier spiritual world.

Praxiteles preceded them, and they entered
the middle hall which was supported by
pillars and open to the sky. Between the
pillars, opposite the entrance, so that it
covered the background, hung a curtain of

rich dark stuff, and before it were placed
sedilia, whereon the guests seated themselves.
The host disappeared behind the curtain,
and forthwith came the soft music of flutes
and of string instruments; the curtain was
silently and slowly drawn aside, and the
guests sat as if transfixed at the inexpressibly
beautiful sight that met their gaze.

In the middle of the chamber, snow-white,
contrasting against the dark background
formed by thick green garlands of flowers
and leaves wreathed round the pillars, stood
the Aphrodite of Praxiteles.

There was a long silent pause; but then
suddenly all sprang from their seats and confused exclamations of admiration made known
the impression the wonderful work of art had
evoked.

The Archons forgot their stately dignity,
the ambassadors their cold reserve, and all
pressed forward round Praxiteles, each wanting to be the first to embrace him and to
press him to his heart; some even went so far
in their enthusiasm as to embrace and kiss

the marble image, so that the artist at last
had laughingly to forbid them.

All was in quickened emotion as the slaves
now appeared, and, while decking the guests
with wreaths of roses, made sign that the
repast was ready.

As they entered the banquet-hall, a fresh
exclamation of wonder and delighted surprise
ran murmuring through the throng.

Towards the background of the room,
directly confronting them as they entered,
ran a range of steps; and on the topmost
stood, with bare arms, a female figure holding forth a two-handled pitcher, while at her
feet, on the steps beneath, reclined a youth
and maiden, each stretching out towards her
a beaker.

The woman's laughing glances, the heightened colours of the youth and maiden, and
the slight thrill that quickened the limbs of
the maiden, revealed that these three shapes
of beauty and grace were not of marble, but
real flesh and blood.

" Aphrodite ! " was murmured among the

guests, for one recognised in the female figure the original of the masterpiece in marble on which they had just been gazing.

"Aphrodite, filling the beakers of Ganymede and Hebe," explained one of the Archons.

"Not Hebe, but Iris !" said another ; "that is the meaning of the light-blue vesture from which she is gazing forth."

Phryne-Aphrodite, bending down the pitcher, filled the outstretched beakers, and the Archons stepped forward to receive the wine-cups.

When the beakers had gone the round of the guests, and each had taken a draught, Phryne sprang down from the pedestal and advanced with merry laugh towards Praxiteles, while Myrtolaos and Hellanodike in like manner rose up.

"Art content ? and have I learned in thy school ? " she asked the sculptor, with sparkling eyes.

" Ye men ot Cnidos," said he, placing his arm round her form, " on returning home

ye may relate that your eyes have rested on
Phryne, upon whom Venus bestowed her own
fair form, and Pallas vouchsafed her intelli-
gence."

"And Praxiteles has lent his magic chisel,"
interrupted she, with touching pride.

Phryne had taken captive the minds and
hearts of all present ; and, as with one voice, it
was resolved that to her pertained the office of
symposiarch, or controller of the feast.   This
post assigned to her the charge of arranging
what seemed likely to inspire the discourse of
the guests and quicken the joy of the banquet;
the spirit of the feast was at her disposal.

With deft address she took up her charge,
and, all wondering, Hellanodike gazed at
her and listened, while sitting apart shy
and reserved in this unwonted presence of
men around.   No one gave her any heed, for
all thought was intent on Phryne.   Myrtolaos
was seated far away from her, at the further
end of the table, and there was but one
among the whole throng whose eyes passed
by Phryne, to rest lingering on Hellanodike.

It was Mnemarch. He uttered few words,
and his silent yearning glances, the more he
was quickened by the glowing wine, grew
ever more ardent. Never had the maiden
looked so beautiful in his sight, never so
worthy of awakening inmost emotion.

When the delights of the table had been
indulged in for long hours, and the excitement of all present had reached its highest
pitch, the fair controller of the feast beckoned
to one of the attendant slaves and whispered
some words. Straightway the doors of the
banqueting-room sprang open, and with
rushing clatter, with flutes and rattling tam-
bourines resounding, poured in a throng of
girls and youths. Every voice forthwith
hushed, every eye was turned to the new
comers, who were ranging themselves for the
dance.

At the outset the tread was measured and
restrained the movements of the dancers, but
soon the interweaving grew wilder, the youths
quickening the pace swung higher their
partners in the dizzy whirl ; some of the

maidens flung loose their hair, while from
others again their partners snatched the fillets
that held back their locks; and so went rushing on the wild crowd, like to a troop of
mœnides, ejaculating and shouting, in reckless
disorder.

The gaze of the guests quickened; Phryne
stood at her full height by the end of the
table, smiling tranquilly, while the wild troop
went whirling by.

" Check your pace," cried she, suddenly, in
clear tones to the tossing crowd, which forthwith obeyed her behest. " Your dance is
too wild," she said, "and the best is still
lacking. Is there not among you one that
can rejoice our eyes by dancing all alone ? "

One of the maidens came forward.

" Fair Phryne," she said, while flinging
back her long hair from her glowing cheeks,
" at other feasts 'tis I who take the lead, but
here I dare not venture."

" Wherefore not here ? "

" Because Phryne is in presence, before
whom skill such as mine must shrink abashed,

for all in Athens know that no one in the dance can compare with her."

The guests sprang from their seats.

" Show us thy skill, Phryne," was the cry. " Phryne must dance."

For a brief space she seemed to waver, but soon after advanced into the room ; youths and maidens alike drew back to make way for her. To one of the flute-players she gave a sign, and to the rhythm he sounded she began, suiting the music, a slow and stately measure. The trailing garment, descending to her feet, hindered any quicker motion, and her dance, in the main, was resolved into a measured tread, a swaying of the body, a graceful rise and fall of the garment. Yet were her movements of such grace that a murmur of delight ran through the surrounding spectators.

" You are too considerate," broke in Phryne with laughter, " if you be content with such slumbrous dance."

" Show us, then, one more joyous," interrupted Praxiteles, heated by wine.

Her eyes gleamed with unwonted fire.

" Bide a while," she cried, and vanished from their presence.

A breathless hush ; murmured whisperings among the guests, and all eyes fixed expectant on the door by which she had passed. Sudden the curtains were flung back, and an exclamation of enraptured wonder broke from every lip.

The outer garment was thrown off, and the fine white woollen under-robe, clinging to her form and bringing into relief the contour, was lifted to the knee, and her sandals were laid aside.

Lithesome as a panther, she sprang among the maidens, and, snatching from the hand of one of them a tambourine, began, while thrumming her accompaniment, a wild bacchante dance.

Every outline of the elastic form displayed a rapture of motion, and as she felt the gaze of the beholders fixed upon her, the enchantment of bygone days came to her anew ; anew she was Phryne of the past, and

their eyes, anon flashing, anon dazed, revealed
how magical was the spell entrancing them ;
forgetful of herself, dizzied with the delighted plaudits that rose from all beholders
alike, ever more rapid whirled on the mazy
measure, closer clung the subtile texture
round the flowing contour, bringing still
more into relief the poetry of her form ;
suddenly the dance was suspended, and while
all were rapt in ecstasy and well-nigh unable
to keep in check, she stood looking upon the
throng with wreathed smiles, all unmoved,
the only being there asserting a full mastery
over herself.

She gave a start, as though shuddering, and
lifted an unsandalled foot from the marble
pavement.

" The ground is cold," she said ;
" I am chilled; from whom may I get
shelter ? "

" Here ! " and " here ! " resounded the
laughing reply from every side, and one
and all stretched forth a pleading arm towards the fair petitioner.

She paid no heed.

"From the handsomest," she exclaimed, with clear, ringing tones, and, straightway, ere the bewildered guests were aware, she leaped on the couch where Myrtolaos was reclining, and nestled down close to the astounded youth.

Hellanodike started half forward from her seat.

Phryne had observed this; with reckless laughter she threw her arms round Myrtolaos, while fixing a look of withering scorn on the maiden.

She caught up the beaker standing near.

"Fill the wine-cups, slaves!" she cried, "and give every youth and maiden here wine, that there be no one in this presence who may look upon the madness of drink with the cold eye of reserve."

The slaves obeyed the behest; Phryne lifted high the wine-cup.

"Hear what the controller of the feast ordains: 'Death to coyness, death to modesty and reserve!'"

" Death to them all ! " broke forth the wild throng in chorus.

" And long live folly, long live blessed madness ! "

" Long live both ! " resounded in reply.

A wild, disorderly bacchanalian scene ensued, and while the revellers whirled in interwoven maze through the mad rout, Phryne bent close her lips to Myrtolaos' ear.

" Listen to me, fair and foolish boy," she whispered in thrilling tones, " to whom I wish well, albeit thou so little givest heed. I see thee suffering and know what fails thee ; thou wouldst fain be an artist like Praxiteles, and mayst not become so because thou hast let thy warm heart get bound to a loved one that is chilling."

Myrtolaos looked at her bewildered and dumbfounded.

" Thou seest that I read thy thoughts," continued Phryne, with an air of triumph. " Well, then, I will aid thee, and will of thee make an artist, and of thy Bœotian, an Athenian."

"What means this?" asked he, wonderingly.

"Thou shalt see," she broke in hurriedly; "let me go on and trouble me not, deem that all happens for thy welfare."

Ere he could snatch the sense of her words she started up from the cushion where she had been lying.

"Be still!" she cried to the maddening crowd, and immediate silence followed.

In clear tones she exclaimed,—"Ye men who know the original after which Praxiteles fashioned the Cnidian Venus, is there among you one who blameth Phryne that she served as model?"

"Whoso would," said one of the envoys from Cnidos, with flattering tone, "him would I despatch to the Paphlagonians, and let him feed on acorns."

"Be not so harsh!" answered Phryne, turning to the envoy, "for thy word might reach a woman, and then would it not be tender."

"A woman?" asked Praxiteles.

" Listen, then," and Phryne's voice grew harsher ; " there is amongst us one who in her heart of hearts curses my act ; the friend of an artist who refuses to her friend what Phryne permitted to hers."

" Whom dost thou mean ? " arose from every side.

" There !—Hellanodike, the daughter of Myronides, from Tanagra."

All eyes turned towards Hellanodike, who, trembling in every limb, sat as upon embers.

" Look at her," went on Phryne ; " saw ye ever a shape that Pallas moulded more after her own form ? "

Myrtolaos started up.

" What art thou about ? " he said half aloud to Phryne.

She laid her hand upon his shoulder and pressed him down laughingly to his seat.

" Yonder sits the ruler in the realm of beauty," she said, pointing to Praxiteles. " Come, then, say whether Art has any

claim on this being, and whether she dare
any longer withstand the claim of Art."

Praxiteles rose laughing from his seat.

" It needs no master in art," he replied,
" to pronounce that this fair form——"

" Pallas ! she must appear as Pallas ! "
broke forth in disorderly cry from
twenty throats. The guests, divining
Phryne's intent, caught at the notion
eagerly.

" Dost hear ? " said Phryne, turning to
Hellanodike ; " thou must obey the in-
junction ; yonder stands Paris,—appear to
him even as did Pallas in presence of
the son of Priam."

"Never ! " she gasped, " never, never ! "

The alarmed girl pressed both arms
against her breast.

" Thou must ! " cried Phryne in strident
tones.

She dashed forward towards Hellanodike, and snatching fast the clasp that
held her garment on her shoulder, loosened
it. In the energy of dismay Hellanodike

sprang forward, pushing back her assailant,
and would fain have fled the hall.

" Bring aid !" cried Phryne to the dancers,
and like to a band of demons they fell upon
Hellanodike, barring her way out.

Then formed around a dense, disorderly
rabble, and her beautiful bewildered eyes
wandered, as if dazed, around her throng of
tormentors, while she sought with convulsive
grasp to hold the garment tight to her
shoulder.

" Hold the Bœotian fast !" shouted suddenly Mnemarch, who had noticed Myrtolaos springing from his couch.

Two bondmen threw themselves upon
him, and, grasping him by the arms and
shoulders, pressed him down with all their
might into his seat.

" Unhand me!" raged Myrtolaos ; yet
they loosened not their grasp, but kept him
fast, as with iron grip.

This was the signal for the breaking loose
from all restraint and bounds.

The female dancers became transformed

into frenzied creatures. They seized Hellanodike by the hands and arms, and a yell
of triumph rent the air as the azure garment,
torn from her shoulders, went fluttering earth-
ward. As a snow drift shining amid the
darksome tumult of sable locks and flushing
cheeks, and in the convulsive strain of her
mortal anguish, she pressed her arms over
her bared bosom, to hold faster still the
falling robe.

Presently Mnemarch, his face wearing the
aspect of a beast of prey, rushed into the
throng, and, making towards Hellanodike,
with one hand grasped her fair arm to bear
down her resistance, with the other seized
her robe, so as with one last snatch to tear
it away.

"Myrtolaos!" rose a trembling bewildered
cry.

Thereupon resounded from the end of the
room a wild bursting yell of agony, and
over the table with a mighty bound came
rushing into the midst of the swaying crowd,
flinging them right and left, a powerful form

that encompassed Hellanodike from behind
with stalwart arm. Next moment it swung
crushing down on Mnemarch's skull, whose
head dropped upon his breast, his hands sank
heavily, and smitten by a stroke of the fist
that seemed dealt as with the force of a
sledge-hammer, he fell headlong to earth,
gasping.

Hoarse, grating tones came murmuring on
Hellanodike's ear. She caught not their
sense, for vehement excitement broke up
the words ere escaping from the lips, but
she recognised the voice, and even amidst
her anxiety and mortal confusion a feeling
of nameless rapture thrilled through her
frame. She twined her arms about his neck,
and clung to him so fast that the quick
throbbings of his heart found echo in her
breast, as she gazed into the beloved eyes
of Myrtolaos.

As with his left hand he clasped her to
him, with the right he seized a wine jar
lying empty on the ground, and swinging it
upward threateningly, poised aloft as a weapon,

and with vibrating lips and gleaming eyes measuring the bystanders, he stood like to a youthful Theseus battling among the Centaurs.

At the further end of the room, crouched on the ground, lay gasping for breath one of the slaves that had held down Myrtolaos, and whom with a fling of his foot he had dashed against the wall.

For a brief space one and all, in dumbfounded bewilderment, had fallen back, and Phryne stood for a while silent amid the rest, wholly bereft of her presence of mind. Her brows frowning loweringly, her hands twitching and twisting convulsively, revealed meanwhile the tempest of wrath that went careering through her spirit. Therewith her glance caught what was passing behind the youth. Mnemarch had come to himself. His first token of returning life was a fierce glance of mortal hate directed against Myrtolaos. That glance escaped not Phryne's keen sight, and straightway she noted how Mnemarch's hand began clutching convul-

sively beneath his robe. She knew what
he sought for, and a dreadful thought pervaded her heart thirsting for vengeance.
She came forward, therefore, to gain time
for Mnemarch, and to prevent Myrtolaos
from looking round at his opponent. Suddenly she stood straight before the youth.

"What art thou venturing on in the
house of Praxiteles?" she cried, and anger
gave to her voice a grating sound. "What
wouldst thou, Bœotian?"

"I am protecting her from thee," was his
reply; and his hand grasped firmer the handle
of the wine jar.

At this instant an incident befel that took
breath and reflection away from all present.

With vehement haste Praxiteles glanced
at Myrtolaos; with colossal strength tore
him away, while, with both arms thrown
around him, he forced him some steps
aside.

"Scoundrel!" he shouted, his voice resounding in thunder tones, and the next
moment he caught by the neck him thus

fitted with the epithet,—Mnemarch, and held him, wriggling like a lizard, high in air.

A long double-edged blade was flashing in Mnemarch's hand, and now, in Praxiteles' iron grip, crunched together, bereft of strength, he let drop the murderous steel to the ground.

The sculptor loosed his hold from his throat, and Mnemarch sank gasping down.

Praxiteles stood over him, a deep fold and sombre, as though indented by the chisel, lay between his eyes, and he looked as if he would lift his foot and crush Mnemarch in the dust. The latter cowered on the ground, and lifted not his gaze.

A deep mortal stillness prevailed in the room; it was as though a lion had burst among the throng and broken into savage roaring.

Hellanodike clung shuddering, like one fever-stricken, to the arm of Myrtolaos.

"Come!" now was whispered hurriedly in her ear from her beloved's voice, "come!"

All unconsciously she clung to him who

now acted and thought for her. The eyes
and ears of all were now bent on Praxiteles
and Mnemarch ; no one observed the two
that now noiselessly slipped away behind the
rest.

Praxiteles now stepped back, and the spell
that held the surrounding bystanders in
breathless suspense was loosed.

Hurriedly, in awe-stricken disorder, the
band of dancers one and all pressed forward
towards the entrance, and the flickering of
torches that slaves now bore in the darkening
room fell on the pallid, troubled faces.

Mnemarch scrambled up from the ground,
and would fain, with sunken head, have
slunk off.

" Take thy knife away!" cried Praxiteles
after him, and at the words resounding in
awe-inspiring tone, Mnemarch turned back,
obedient as a hound, snatched up the knife
from the ground, and slunk forth.

Phryne had silently vanished whilst the
tumult was in full swing

" Come ! let us go out from hence," said

he, in a low voice, for he felt how her body, protected only from the night air by the light festive garment, trembled in his arms.

"No," said she, "I do not feel the cold;" and she walked close by him with twofold speed.

A few hundred steps they might have walked thus, and had just turned the corner of the road, when they heard somebody rushing after them, breathless and panting.

Hellanodike shuddered.

" Onward !" said Myrtolaos, and he pushed on.

"Not by this way," she heard whispered close to her ear.

" Chlenusa !" said both as with one breath; the next moment she was at their side. The long dark cloak which covered her from head to foot fluttered behind her.

" Why not this way ? " asked Myrtolaos ; " is not this the way to the northern gate? "

" They are behind," she said, breathlessly, "you will fall into their hands."

" Who pursues us ? " asked Myrtolaos.

" Timoessa with her slaves—come in here !"

Uttering these words, she grasped the hand of Myrtolaos, and with the energy of despair drew him into a side street, which yawned dark and narrow before them.

"On, on!" she cried, seeing that Myrtolaos wanted to pause ; and the sound of her half stifled voice seemed to indicate so alarming a peril that the youth followed without further ado. The street had no outlet, and they could not advance further.

"Remain here and do not stir," said Chlenusa ; "and thou take this," turning to Hellanodike, while she tore the cloak from her own shoulders and put it round the trembling girl ; "the night is cold, and you have still far to go."

"But thou?" asked Hellanodike.

"I need my cloak no more." There was deep anguish in her voice. "Farewell, and farewell, farewell!" And while she sought Hellanodike's face in the darkness, she kissed her with every word on mouth, and cheek, and eyes. Then quitting them she hastened from the side street back to the high road.

The same moment a dull thud of heavy
footsteps came round the corner of the
road, a gleam of light was thrown into the
side street, and Timoessa, accompanied by
two slaves bearing torches, appeared at the
opening of the street.

The smouldering gleam of the torches lit
up with a deep red glow the vicious face of
the old hag and the savage features of the
slaves. One of the latter bore a coil of
ropes slung round his arm, a naked sword
was glittering in the other's hand. They
halted near the street, and the sound of
their quickened breath could be heard afar
off.

" They have left the road," said one of
the slaves ; "and yet I had seen them before
us all the while."

"Then they have noticed us and are
hidden somewhere here," cried Timoessa ;
" let us hunt for them !"

Hellanodike sank on Myrtolaos' breast, and
he also felt a cold shudder passing through
his limbs.

Of a sudden he who bore the sword came up.

" Look there ! " he exclaimed, and from the other side of the street came forward Chlenusa within range of the torchlight.

Like a vulture swooped Timoessa on the maiden.

" Where are they bestowed ? Thou knowest ! " she shrieked, and her hands fastened round the neck of the girl.

Chlenusa sank on her knees.

" Wilt thou speak ? " demanded the slave who, with the sword ready to smite, came close to her, every thew of the sinewy arm thrilling with murderous intent.

" Spare my life ! " returned Chlenusa ; " I will confess all. You are on the wrong track, they are there yonder," and she pointed in quite the contrary direction, " right round the Acropolis ; they are seeking to wend back to Praxiteles' house ; I have warned them."

" Warned them ! " screamed Timoessa. "Speed after them ! " she said, turning to the slaves, " catch them, seize them ! should they

11

reach Praxiteles' house, they are lost to us !"

"And this one here?" asked the slave, holding his sword over Chlenusa.

"Give thy cord hither," said Timoessa. She tore from his arm one of the bonds he bore, and, aided by the slave, threw Chlenusa on the ground.

"With her we will settle the reckoning later on," she screamed, while she pressed with her knees on the back of the girl, and fastened her hands behind her.

"Away, after them ! and when they are caught, bring them both hither !"

The slaves turned, and like two panthers breathing slaughter rushed away through the street fronting them.

Timoessa lingered behind, kneeling on Chlenusa; the weighed-down breast of the martyred girl gave forth a half-suffocated sigh.

"Have pity !" she groaned ; "art thou not my mother ?"

"I thy mother ?" and Timoessa's teeth

gnashed against each other; "in the street I found thee and picked thee up, thou——"

She was unable to finish, for a heavy grasp plunged suddenly out of the dark, and was planted like a bolt of iron on her contorted mouth.

She would fain have screamed out, but only a gurgling sound was audible; she would fain have sprung up, but held fast by the sturdy grasp on her neck, she whirled round upon herself, and fell to the ground with a crash.

On the moment, a tatter was torn from her garment and stuck in her mouth as a gag; next instant the knots were loosed from Chlenusa's hands, and while till now all had gone forward in awful silence, Timoessa now heard a well-known voice quickened with wrath.

"Knowst thou me, go-between, thou bird of prey accurst? take that and that, and bear this to Mnemarch," and at the same time came rattling down the cord swung by Myrtolaos' hand in wrathful whizzing strokes on her face, and hands, and

shoulders. His wrath foamed like a raging
torrent from his heart, and he lashed out
upon her until howling she writhed upon
the ground, and cord as well as pavement
was besprinkled with her blood.

At last he flung the instrument of
punishment at Timoessa, and bent down
to Chlenusa.

"Canst thou stand?" he asked.

She raised herself, aided by his arm,
with difficulty from the ground.

"Come," he said, "thou goest with us;"
and he lifted up in his arms the slender form.

Hellanodike took hold of the hand of
Chlenusa as it drooped down, and a soft
smile played around the lips of the pitiable
being. A few paces and the town-gate
was reached, and they went forth in freedom.
They breathed with laboured breath,—they
were safe.

The solemn stillness of night encompassed them around, and overhead glistened
the immortal stars; to the north, in the
direction about where Tanagra lay, hung

a brilliant star, shimmering in soft tremulous
light.

" Whither away now ? " asked Hellanodike gently, as Myrtolaos stood still, and
let Chlenusa softly down from his arms.

" To thy father," he returned.

Thereupon she fell upon his neck, and
her silent tears mingled with his.

A few days had gone by.

Still and sultry hung the midday sun
above the mountain of Tanagra, the houses
of the town flared in the blinding light,
and like unto so many staring eyes peered
forth from amid the silent landscape at
their feet.

And now they perceived how on the
edge of the olive grove there below, lying
like a green-shaded island in the midst
of the sun-burnt fields, a figure appeared,
a fair, slim, maidenly shape, how she drew
the broad shading hat deeper over her face,
that the sun rays should not prevent her
from gazing across at the well-known and

beloved walls and gates; and the houses
of Tanagra had become aware of her presence, and had they been able would have
given mutual greeting and whispered,—

"She is there once more,—she, whom we
held in our strong embrace, and who flitted
away from us so thoughtlessly,—our darling
Hellanodike."

Other eyes still had observed Hellanodike
while she stood thus on the border of the
grove, haloed in the light which, with the sun's
rays and leafy shade intermingled, encompassed her; and those eyes had with more
earnest tenderness and sadness rested on her.
Behind her, on the border of a brook that
hurried through the wood, sat Myrtolaos
and gazed on her, and tired not of gazing,
for he knew that to-day it was for the
last time. When it was dark he would
take her to Tanagra, and to the house of
Myronides, for they were coy of the day-
light. How had he once dreamed of returning to this house, and how had he come
back in reality! A bitter pain pierced his

heart, and in gloomy thoughts he bowed
down his head.

A light footfall sounded behind him,—
Hellanodike touched his shoulder.

"Chlenusa has not yet returned," she
said ; "she wanted to pluck blackberries
for us. I am tired out from our day's
journey."

"Rest thyself," he replied ; "I will watch
over thee."

On the grassy bank of the brook Hellanodike lay herself down ; he heaped leaves
and moss under her head, that she might
rest more softly, and he sat down by her
side. Like to a child that, while sinking
to rest, stretches out its grasp for the
cherished toy, she took hold of his hand,
and with eyes weighing down with sleep,
once more gave a kindly glance, and was
sunk in slumber.

He sat near her and gazed down upon
her. The sight of her native town had
endowed anew the features of the noble
countenance with the innocent charm of

youth, and the memories of the last terrible days lay spread thereon as with a far-cast shadow.

Then his eyes fell upon the water that went plashing at his feet, and look yonder, there, under the clear current, there gleamed a layer of the finest yellowish-brown clay.

"How well might that be worked up and shaped!" he thought to himself, and got angered as he found himself dallying with the thought, for the strife was now at an end; he was conscious that he was not born to be an artist.

Yet the force of old habit seized him; he carefully loosed his hold of the tiny hand still lying in his own, and, half sunk in thought, he took some clay from the streamlet's bed. He felt the soft moist material in his hand, looked down at Hellanodike, who, softly breathing, lay reclined before him in deep slumber, so that it looked as though she wished to give him ample time to take in every contour of her figure, every lineament of her countenance, by way of

lasting remembrance. Suddenly, in spite of
reason, the old delight seized his very soul,
and he determined, by his last handiwork, to
fashion a memorial of his beloved. It was
not to be a statue such as came from Praxiteles' hands, and such as he had in vain
attempted with painful effort to shape,—
nothing more than an image of Hellanodike;
but like, so like as he could possibly make it,
in every fold of the drapery, with the broad-
brimmed hat which she loved so much to
wear, and with that smile which now so
mysteriously hovered over her sweet face, as
though a rapturous dream had told her of
unlooked-for joy and content.

In the posture he had seen her assume
when watching her on the borders of the
olive grove, looking over towards Tanagra,
he determined to represent her, and without
tarrying set to work.

As he commenced working, inmost happiness filled his heart, such as he had never
known ; all sorrow of bygone hours and all
cares of the future were forgotten; a soft

gentle breeze passed through the green
wood ; and it seemed to him as though
the minor deities of the woods and of love
sprang up from behind the trees and stood
around him, and, softly whispering, looked
over his shoulder at his work.   And now, as
the shapeless clay assumed the form of a
slender figure, and each impression and
stroke of his hand seemed to exercise a magic
spell and to impart fresh, warm life into the
graceful body and into the drapery which
flowed around her form;   and when at
last, in small proportions, yet perfectly
recognisable, Hellanodike's sweet features
appeared, he had to check himself not to
burst out in loud, joyous exclamation ;   he
only murmured her name quite softly and
gazed at her, and saw that she still was rapt
in dreams, and that she still smiled, and an
invincible desire overcame him to wake her
with a kiss; yet he did not do so, for she
must still sleep on till the figure was quite
finished.   Thus he continued working and
working ;   to each fold of the delicate gar-

ment he gave its place, each wavelet of dark-
brown locks he marked with the sharpened
point of a twig, which he had cut to suit his
purpose, and thus he did not notice how
someone came behind him tripping through
the wood. It was Chlenusa, who had been
looking for blackberries, and was returning
with her woodland plunder. When she had
come quite close he noticed her, and laid his
finger on his lips, in sign not to wake Hellanodike from her slumbers; then he showed
her the little figure, which was now completed.
She took it up with a look of indifference ;
but scarcely had she gazed at it, when her
face changed, her dark eyes flashed, and
" Hellanodike ! Hellanodike !" she cried,
dancing round the sleeping form in wild joy.
Myrtolaos wanted to restrain her, but Hellanodike had already awoke and looked
about her in astonishment. Chlenusa rushed
to her and seated herself on the sward beside
her.

"Dost thou know who this is? Dost thou
know her ?" she exclaimed, in joy and

laughter, showing her the image; and in
amazement Hellanodike regarded her own
sweet features.

"Myrtolaos," she said, "hast thou made
it?"

Chlenusa clapped her hands. "He has
made it," she said; "he who has been
asleep till now, and has only this day
awakened." She snatched the figure from
Hellanodike's hands, and pressed it to her
bosom.

"Thou wilt crush it," said Myrtolaos.

"I crush it?" the girl replied; "dost
think I could spoil such?"

With a single bound she was at the nearest
olive bush, tore off a branch, and twisted it
into the shape of a wreath. Almost solemnly
she approached Myrtolaos.

"Give ear," she said, "when they shall
once crown thee with the wreath sacred in all
Hellas, then forget not that it was Chlenusa
who first crowned thee."

The girl was as it were in a rapture, and
Myrtolaos was not sure whether her strange,

passionate words were in earnest or jest. Meantime he did not restrain her from standing on tip-toe, and pressing the olive wreath on his dark locks.

Chlenusa turned to Hellanodike.

"Is he alone to be crowned?" she said; "wait, I will weave thee a wreath of wild roses."

"Roses in an olive grove?" he asked.

"If not in the wood, then on the borders of it," she replied. "Come, I had picked blackberries for you, do you eat while I am seeking."

"Leave the figure here," Myrtolaos called out to her, as she was hastening away. But she swung it high above her head, holding it up like a trophy, laughing the while, and soon disappeared in the copse.

Hellanodike and Myrtolaos sat close together, side by side, and partook of the berries, of which the girl had brought them a large heap; they spoke not, for their thoughts were cast down, reflecting on the coming hours.

As Myrtolaos had prophesied, Chlénusa
found no roses in the wood, nor on the
borders of it, where she had roved up and
down ; but in the plain between town and
wood her keen eyes fancied they had discovered the sought-for prize. She hurried in
the direction along the road, and only when
she was quite close to the rose bushes did
she notice that a moat and enclosure separated her from them.

For the light-footed girl this obstacle was
small ; without a moment's hesitation she
leaped over the moat, climbed over the
enclosure, and plucked a whole lapful of
roses.

In the midst of her occupation ponderous
footsteps came trudging along, and of a
sudden she felt her arm ungently seized by
a rough grip.

" So I have caught thee, thou thieving
wench," said the gardener; "dost not see
that this is a garden and private property,
in which creatures such as thou have no
business ?"

"I am no thief," said the girl, and tried vainly to wriggle out of his clutches.

"Thou no thief?" and he looked at the bronzed, gipsy creature, who certainly had much resemblance to a tramp. "Come thou with me, we will give thee thorns for thy roses."

He dragged her along with him, and only now did she notice that she was in a large, beautifully laid-out garden.

Along one of the broad, cleanly-swept paths a man of noble bearing approached. His hair and beard were very grey, and he walked, as it seemed, sunk in deep thought. As he saw the two advancing towards him, he raised his head.

"Whom dost thou bring with thee there?" he asked of the gardener.

From the submissive demeanour with which the latter stood before him, Chlenusa recognised that he was the owner of the garden.

"Master," said the gardener, "this is plainly one belonging to the bands of

thieves, who of late have made this neigh-
bourhood so unsafe ; I caught her openly
thieving."

" Not thieving, master," the girl exclaimed ;
" I only plucked a few roses from the bushes
in thy garden ; thy garden will be none the
poorer thereby."

To confirm her words she spread out the
folds of her dress, and let the roses fall to
the ground ; at the same moment the little
image also fell, which she had been carrying,
covered by the roses, in her lap.

Hurriedly she bent down to catch it, but
the gardener was quicker than she.

" Thou thieving magpie," he cried in
triumph, " is that a rose too ? "

The girl burst into tears.

" Do not handle it so roughly and un-
couthly ! " she called out to the gardener ;
" dost thou not see, thou uncouth one, that
thou art spoiling it ? "

The owner of the garden grew attentive.

" What is that ? " he asked, and took the
image from the hands of his servant. But

scarcely had he glanced at it than the tall figure trembled with emotion.

" Whence hast thou this ? " he asked, " where is she whom this represents ? "

The girl looked up at him with dark, glistening eyes, and remained silent.

" Dost thou not hear what the master asks thee ? " grumbled the gardener, interrupting.

"If thou dost know her, and dost bear malice against her," Chlenusa replied slowly, " thou shalt kill me ere I tell thee where to find her."

He placed his one hand on her black flowing locks, whilst with the other he pressed with tender care the little figure to his heart.

" Lead me to her," said he, "and fear not ! "

Chlenusa felt the hand laid on her head trembling slightly.

The shades of the trees were lengthening in the wood; Myrtolaos looked up to the sky, and heaved a deep sigh.

" It grows late," said he; "when we arrive

12

at Tanagra it will be dark; we must hurry, otherwise they will not let us enter the town gates.   Come, Hellanodike."

She fastened her hat on her head, and her heart was throbbing with excitement; meanwhile he approached the brook, picked Chlenusa's olive wreath to pieces, and let leaf by leaf float down, drawn on by the gentle current.

"Dost thou not rejoice that we return to my father?" she asked, placing her arm on his shoulder.

He turned round to her with heavy heart.

"Thou dost return to him," he replied,— " not I."

She grew pale, and he twined his arm about her.

"Myrtolaos!" she cried, in astonishment and alarmed, for in her simplicity she had never thought of such eventuality.

"No," said he, "when I fled from him together with thee and brought shame on his grey hair, I was but a lad; now I have learnt what a man feels when wrong is done to what he loves best, and that a man cannot forgive it. Come,"—he did not utter her name, for he feared that the sweet sound of it would break down all his courage,—" we must now part from each other here."

Sobbing she lay on his breast. It seemed to her as if her whole previous life was merged in a black fathomless depth, and Tanagra without him was no longer Tanagra to her.

" Oh that Praxiteles had never come to us!" she murmured.

"Be silent," he said, in tremulous tones, "be silent; do not mention his name any more, thou dost rend my heart."

Thus they stood, her head close to his, both so young, so beautiful, yet so unhappy; by nature made for each other, yet by fate torn asunder.

Suddenly a voice was heard behind them, at sound of which they both sprang up trembling.

"Hellanodike!"

The sound was solemn and sorrowful, and looking round they beheld the majestic figure of Myronides standing a few steps apart from them between the trees irradiated by the red light.

"Father!" cried the girl, and in that moment all was forgotten, and she hung round his neck and kissed him with over-flowing tears.

He bent back her head, and looked earnestly and searchingly into her face; but on seeing her eyes turned frankly towards him, he was conscious that she was still his own child, his pure, guileless child, and almost against his will a smile passed over his stern features.

With face averted, and dejected in mind, Myrtolaos had stood apart; Myronides now called him.

As if stunned he advanced a few paces, and then remained standing still.

"Thou art afraid of me, Myrtolaos," said Myronides; and at the sound of his voice, which had pervaded his whole life like a sweet perfume, his heart sank within him; he fell at his feet, and covered Myronides' hand with kisses and tears.

"Look at this," said Myronides, and he
showed the astonished youth the little image
of Hellanodike ; " hast thou made this ? "

Myrtolaos blushed, silently nodding assent.

" Didst thou make it in Athens ? "

" No," replied Myrtolaos, " here in the
forest a few hours ago."

With moist eyes the old man gazed at
the youth, his hand rested lovingly on his
curly head, and he bent low down towards
him.

"Then it is not necessary to live in Athens
in order to create such things ?   I know," he
whispered to him, " thou didst not intend
to return to my house.   Come back to me,
Myrtolaos, my son!"

" My father," stammered the youth, "canst
thou forgive what I have done to thee ? "

" Must I not do so," said Myronides, " as
thou bringest with thee such an ally ? " and
he pointed at Hellanodike's image.

A cry of joy arose from two happy beings,
and Myrtolaos and Hellanodike embraced
the noble man.

" Unloose me," he said, smiling; " here is still someone who awaits me."

He turned round and beckoned to Chlenusa, who had shyly remained in the background, seated on a felled tree.

" The roses that thou didst wish to pick to-day," he said, " are lost ; from henceforth thou shalt pluck as many roses as thou wilt in the garden of Myronides ; thou art now a Tanagrian damsel."

She gazed at him one moment as if she did not understand, for the language of a father's heart was strange to the lonely girl ; suddenly, however, she seemed to apprehend, hurried towards Hellanodike, and throwing herself at her feet on the sward, broke forth into sobs and cries of joy, and pressed her quivering face in the folds of her dress.

Hellanodike bent down and kissed her, and recalled the hours when she had known no comfort and no friend save the wild brown girl.

A year had gone by, when Praxiteles,

entering his studio where his pupils were at
work, found the latter in excited converse.
They crowded round Polymachron, and
seemed to be regarding some object which he
held in his hands.

" What have you there ? " asked the
sculptor.

" Thou shalt decide, master," replied
Polymachron. " We are discussing the worth
of these objects ; at all events, they appear to
us new and original."

He made over to Praxiteles several little
figures in baked clay, which represented
female figures in various positions, some
standing, some as it were walking, some
seated on a rock. The figures were draped,
and the colours of the garments, amongst
which sky-blue was predominant, were
delicately marked.

Praxiteles took the strange little figures in
his hands and regarded them. Suddenly his
gaze grew more intent ; without a word he
quitted the studio. The pupils, left to themselves, looked at each other in astonishment.

With hasty steps he entered his own work-
room, placed the little figures on a table at
the foot of the Hermes model, which for a
long time seemed not to have been touched,
and sat down before it.

For a long time he remained lost in deep
thought, and whoever saw him sitting thus
might have thought that he was reading the
figures.

In truth, it was not much else; for the
little figures before him told him a history
of troubles and sorrows, crowned at last by
the reward of patience, and he listened to
this revelation which filled his heart like a
sweet and luscious fairy tale.

The figures did not vary much in shape,
for it was ever but one face, one form that
repeated itself over and over again; it was
Hellanodike, but love's fantasy played around
the figure, and transformed it into ever
new, ever more charming attitudes; and the
longer he looked, the warmer grew the smile
on the bewitching little face, the more brimful of life every movement of the delicate

limbs, and he felt as if he could hear her
speak, ever only one word, but varying in
all the different strains which love has contrived for human expression, " Myrtolaos,
Myrtolaos ; " and suddenly he sprang up,
and felt that he stood in the midst of
the Paradise which had been created on
earth by the spirit of the great artist,
and the name of this great master was—
Myrtolaos.

" Hermes of Tanagra," said he, as he
stood before the unfinished model of his
favourite pupil who had fled, " then I was
not deceived when for the first time I looked
in thine eyes—and so long hadst thou to
seek till thou didst find what was even so
near to thee ? "

The pupils looked up as Praxiteles returned to them with earnest and almost
solemn demeanour.

" Youths," he said, " I have news for
you ; a master in our art has arisen in Greece ;
it is he whose works Polymachron has shown
me."

A surprised whisper ran through the throng.

" Who can it be ? " asked Polymachron.

" I think we know him," said Praxiteles. " From whom have you these figures ? "

" From a girl who seemed to have come from country parts, and who, as she said, wished to offer the images for sale in the studio of Praxiteles."

" Perhaps it was from her ? " asked Praxiteles, pointing to Chlenusa, who entered at that moment to know the result of her coming.

" To be sure they were from her."

Praxiteles beckoned to the girl.

" I think we know one another ; and so it is thou who dost sell the works of Myrtolaos in Athens ? "

" Myrtolaos ?   Myrtolaos made that ? " ran from mouth to mouth with the rapidity of lightning.

" Ask her," returned Praxiteles, smiling.

" Yea, Myrtolaos in Tanagra," Chlenusa now exclaimed, looking proudly round her. " In Tanagra now everybody crowds towards

the house of Myronides, in which he lives
and works, for all wish to have a figure of
his workmanship. And because he is a
dreamer and does not know what to do to
become a celebrated man, I have got away
without his knowledge, in order to show them
to you, who understand such things."

All laughed, for she looked so quaint in
her self-undertaken mission.

" So thou wilt make him renowned ? " said
Praxiteles.

" Verily," she replied, " for so have I promised Hellanodike."

" Come with me," said he.

He took the girl with him into his studio,
sat down once more before the images, and
everything that these had already told him,
the whole story of their love and happiness
and rich artistic creations, he heard again from
the lips of this dark maiden.

She drew to a close.

" So they are man and wife ? " said he,
" and—why dost thou blush ? "

" Well, it is quite natural," she answered ;

" and he is so pretty, and is so like both of
them."

Praxiteles smiled, and stood before the
Hermes. A thought flashed through his
mind; it must be a happy thought, for it
lighted up his noble brow

" Thou must stay at my house this night,"
he said, turning to Chlenusa, " for thou
knowest Mnemarch still lives. To-morrow
we drive together to Tanagra."

She understood him, and withdrew.

From that moment till the next day,
Praxiteles worked again with the dashing
joyousness of old which had failed him for
so long ; he himself scarce knew why.

But what he had created he hid carefully
under protecting covering, as early the
next morning, accompanied by Chlenusa, he
mounted the chariot.

And once again, as of yore, the car whirled
along the highway from Athens to Oropos,
and from Oropos in the direction of Tanagra ;
once more the Eubœan Sea splashed close by
on the strand and drifted towards the dark-

haired man and his companion the refreshing
breath of its foaming billows; and again the
goad descended quicker and quicker on the
backs of the horses, the nearer they approached to the end of their journey. He
drew up with loud rattle at the door of
Myronides, hasty steps resounded through
the house, and in the next moment a loud and
joyous cry was heard from the studio, where
the young sculptor had been engaged at his
work, and Myrtolaos was clasped in the arms
of his beloved master.

Through the widely-opened doors of the
studio one could look into the green and
flowery garden, and over the threshold came,
attracted by the joyous cry, the other inmates
of the house.

Myronides, whose hair had grown whiter,
and whose step more languid, was never-
theless the first to greet the guest; and then
a slight rustling noise was heard passing the
threshold, and, blushing in sweet confusion,
the lovely young mother Hellanodike entered
the apartment. With her came a fourth

young inmate of the house, not yet known
of Praxiteles, who from out his mother's arms
reached towards the kindly and majestic
man, till he took him smilingly from Hellanodike, and made him ride on his arms.

Myrtolaos advanced.

" Look at this dear little fellow," said he,
" he seems to know that he bears thy name."

" Oh, ye happy ones," said Praxiteles,
restoring the little boy to his mother's arms,—
" there is nothing one can give you, for you
possess all ! And yet permit that I come
not with empty hands into the midst of your
abundance."

At a sign given, a servant fetched the
mysterious object he had brought with him
from Athens; before the eyes of the expectant beholders he detached the coverings
and an exclamation of surprise was heard.

Before them stood, executed on a small
scale, the finished model of Hermes.

It was the one of old, yet different withal,
for the gloomy-looking Hermes had become
transformed into a genially-dreamy Hermes,

on whose left arm a charming boy was
swaying, and the uplifted right of the deity
bore no longer the staff with which he guides
the dead to the shades below, but a full
bursting cluster of grapes, which he dangled
enticingly before the eyes of the sportive
child.

"And now," said Praxiteles smiling, "let
us to business!"

They all looked at him in wonderment.

"Yes," he went on, "thou must name
the price I may purchase these at," and he
drew from the folds of his garment the little
images Chlenusa had brought to Athens.

"Thou knowest them?" cried Myrtolaos.

"More than that," returned Praxiteles,
"I possess them, never more to let them
go from me."

"Myronides," said he with earnest voice,
as he laid his arms round Myrtolaos and
Hellanodike's shoulders and advanced with
them towards his host, "I tore this young
sapling from thy garden, and it came about
as thou saidst, the soil remained clinging to

his roots ; he hath tasted of foreign land and foreign sun, and if to him it proved too hot and too vivid, the pains he thereby endured were health-giving, since they taught him to know the ground he needed to unfold his genius. Be happy, Myronides, thou wilt not lose him more, for nearest to thy heart is the spot where this noble sapling must strike root, so that he may take growth. And grow he will," he exclaimed with enthusiasm ; " and if this town should ever vanish from earth, yet there will hover over its ruins like unto a sweet dream of bygone days, the spirit of him who fashioned these works, the spirit of the Master of Tanagra."

As all separated late in the evening, to betake themselves to rest, Myrtolaos and Praxiteles stood for a moment alone.

" And Phryne ? " inquired Myrtolaos.

" Speak not of her," said Praxiteles ; " she now dwells at Rhodos—with Apelles."

Printed by Hazell, Watson, & Viney, Ld., London and Aylesbury.